Yes, I'm a Tramp

Les Goodwin was born in 1924 and began his career as a bookkeeper for Twentieth Century Fox Film Company, which was based at Morton Pinkney Manor, Warwickshire. After the war he returned to Lancashire, trained as a physiotherapist and remained in private practice until he retired.

Les has been an avid follower of greyhound racing and his four-footed friends have provided him with many years of enjoyment. His love for the 'dogs' prompted him to write his first book 'Dog Tails'. This, his second work, shows the same twinkling sense of earthy humour tinged with a bit of anarchy. A third book based on his experiences as a physiotherapist is well advanced.

He lives in a stone cottage in a picturesque Pennine village in Saddleworth with his wife Irene, Kate the dog and Beauty the cat.

Yes, I'm a Tramp

by

Les Goodwin

Jade Publishing Limited,
5, Leefields Close, Uppermill, Oldham, Lancashire, OL3 6LA.

This first impression published by Jade Publishing Limited 1999.

© Les Goodwin 1999 All rights reserved.

ISBN 1-900734-16-8
Yes, I'm a Tramp.
First impression.

Typeset by
Jade Publishing Limited, Uppermill, Oldham, Lancashire.

British Library Cataloguing in Publication Data
Goodwin, Les, 1924–
  Yes, I'm a Tramp
  First impression
  I. Title
  823. 9 ' 14 [F]

ISBN 1-900734-16-8

This book is sold subject to condition that it shall not, by way of trade or otherwise, be lent, re-sold, hired out, or otherwise circulated without the publisher's prior consent in any form of binding or cover other than that in which it is published and without a similar condition including this condition being imposed on the subsequent purchaser. No part of this publication may be reproduced, stored in a retrieval system, or transmitted, in any form or by any means, electronic, mechanical, photocopying, recording or otherwise, without the prior written permission of the publisher.

Contents

		Page
Prologue		ix
Chapter 1	Many a Good Tune Played…	1
Chapter 2	Coffee, Two Sugars	7
Chapter 3	I Fell in Lust	11
Chapter 4	Living with Redundancy	15
Chapter 5	I Head for the Open Road	19
Chapter 6	Norman's Tale	23
Chapter 7	Two Bottles of Gold Top	33
Chapter 8	Those Were the (Dog) Days	37
Chapter 9	Morris the Menace	47
Chapter 10	Where Are They Now?	53
Chapter 11	Don't Pity Me	59
Chapter 12	Frank's Tale	63
Chapter 13	A Load of Old Cobblers	69
Chapter 14	Stud Farm – Help Wanted	73
Chapter 15	Halfway House	79
Chapter 16	Real Men Don't Cry	89
Chapter 17	The Inconsiderate Sod	95
Chapter 18	The Little People	103
Chapter 19	Dead Men's Shoes	111
Chapter 20	Fear	115
Chapter 21	Full Circle	123

Prologue

The view from my seat on the dry-stone wall was wondrous. Poking through the early morning mist that lay like a floaty silk scarf over the valley was the tall chimney of the woollen mill, not coughing smoke on this quiet Sunday morning but standing quietly aloof from the stone cottages that lived in its shadow. Beneath the camouflage of the mist, small creatures hurried about their business, safe in the cover this early brume afforded, for even the sharp eyes and speed of attack of the kestrel hovering above me were of no advantage to him today.

On the other side of the valley, the Pennines rose steeply again, not yet purple with the heather that would colour them in a few weeks' time.

For some unknown reason, my thoughts drifted to Edna. She'd not been a bad wife really, though I, like most men, was guilty of taking my wife for granted. I suppose I imagined that after twenty uneventful years of wedlock, life would go on in much the same way.

It had come as a shock when she'd announced her intention to leave – partly, if I admit it, because I couldn't imagine any man being interested in her. But then I had overlooked her inheritance – not a fortune, but enough to tempt an out-of-work window cleaner.

I imagined once my redundancy money had run out, we would dip into this little windfall that Edna had acquired on the death of her parents (and forthwith opened an Abbey National account in her own name). Was it unreasonable of me to expect that once she had helped to spend all my money, we should then share hers? Obviously it was.

The kestrel gave up ... but too soon. For within minutes of his departure the mist evaporated into a mild morning and the village below woke up to the sound of bells.

I bent and fastened my boot laces tightly. I loaded my rucksack onto my back and without a backwards glance I made for the path on the other side of the dry-stone wall that led to the Pennine Way.

* * * *

But I did not get far on that Sunday. The day turned out fine and I was happy to stop off along the way and lie on my back on the mossy peat listening to nature chattering – water escaping from the earth and trickling over stones down to join a stream, lapwings pee-witting, sheep bleating.

On such a night after such a day, I need not look for shelter nor even bother to unpack the shabby little tent rolled up and strapped to my rucksack. I was happy to sleep under the stars with my head poking out from my sleeping bag and my woolly hat pulled down over my ears.

What is a tramp? A down-and-out, a vagrant, a malingerer, an alcoholic, a substance abuser? I am none of these things, yet there are those who would describe me thus. Myself, I am a traveller, a gentleman of the road. I wash each day, in streams or in public house toilets; I have two sets of clothing, one on and one in the wash; I do not steal, I do not beg ... but if you prefer – yes, I am a tramp.

CHAPTER 1

Many a Good Tune Played...

The mist cleared to make way for yet another fine day – three on the run. Below in the valley, women in overalls were making their way noisily to work at the weaving shed. In an hour or so men in black suits would be making their way to the office. I had once been one of their number, but now I did not envy any of them.

* * * *

"May I?" the man asked, making himself comfortable beside me on the dry-stone wall. He was middle-aged and well dressed.

"I parked my car up the road, too lovely a day to work, if I had any work." He put his briefcase on the ground against the wall, smoothed his hand down the back of his jacket, and pinching his trousers at the knees tugged at them as he sat down ... as he had done every day for the past twenty-five years when he sat down at his desk at the office. Old habits die hard. Patting his knees he addressed me without looking at me.

"I was Chief Accountant with the Gas Board – gave 'em the best part of my life, I did, and then what do they do?" He didn't wait for a reply but carried on "... made me redundant, that's what they did. Haven't told the wife yet. Thought I'd get more sympathy from the girlfriend so I told her first – all she did was moan, 'How can you take me to Malta now?' As if that was all I had to worry about." The man crossed his legs and leant back. "Wife thinks I'm at the office," he said miserably, "three weeks ago it happened."

Now he turned and looked at me – stared at me – eyed me up and down in fact. I knew exactly what he was thinking ... just another tramp, how on earth could *he* understand ...?

"Happens to us all sooner or later," I said.

"Do you mean ...?" he began.

"Right first time," I told him. He looked me up and down.

"Don't think me rude, but .." he paused again, staring at me once more, "... couldn't you find work?"

"Didn't look," I told him truthfully, "fancied a bit of freedom – life on the move – see how the other half lives... anyway, are you happy with *your* life?"

"Not much."

"Well I'm well happy with mine."

I saw a glimmer of light dawning in his eyes.

"It may interest you to know that this tramp you see before you – me – was once Chief Accountant too." I carried on, "Worked for a firm that made toilet paper, deodorised paper, you could say we made the world a sweeter-smelling place. Like you at the time I was pretty miserable, believing I'd given 'em more than they deserved. But actually, being made redundant was the best thing that ever happened to me."

The man reached down for his briefcase and took from it a pack of sandwiches in a Tupperware box. He took off the lid and held the box out to me.

"Do you fancy a sandwich?" he asked.

"Don't mind if I do," I said.

Tucking into the ham and pickle muffin gratefully, I noticed he was fiddling about with his, not attempting to eat it.

"Cheer up, mate," I told him, helping myself to another of his wife's excellent sandwiches. "I could tell you a tale or two. Yes, I'm a tramp – thanks to the Managing Director who made me redundant. I should send him a thank-you letter – the foul-smelling old git!"

Yes, every Monday morning for the past ten years I had kissed the gold lettering on my office door. My title of "Chief Accountant" filled me with pride.

What the hell does he want now? I had grumbled when he had called me to his office. Then when he informed me he was promoting me to "Chief Accountant", I could have kissed him, but I held my gratitude in check and kissed young Molly Middleton on the stairs instead. She wasn't surprised – I often kissed her.

I wasn't a real accountant – not trained as such, not like Percy Longbottom, FCA – but I'd worked in the Accounts Department for five years.

Harry Moreton turned green when he heard of my promotion. He'd been with the firm longer than I had and assumed he would be the obvious choice for the job when old Percy Longbottom finally retired. Unfortunately for him, the Managing Director didn't agree.

When Percy went into hospital for long-overdue attention to his piles, he fell in love with a nurse. It's hard to imagine anyone falling in love with a patient after peering up his rectum for considerable periods of time, but apparently Percy's ardour was reciprocated – so he promptly announced his intention to take early retirement, wed the woman and whisked her off to Spain on his pension.

Still, I digress ....

I didn't like Ronald Higgins much but, nonetheless, he was the Managing Director so I always treated him with respect – I suppose you could say I was a bit of a creep. Like my old dad used to say, "If at first you don't succeed, creep."

From the very start he had put me in my place.

"Fraternising with the female staff is frowned upon," he had pontificated – wasn't long before I found out why – the female staff didn't call him "Randy Ronald" for nothing – he was the biggest lecher in the firm – and didn't like competition! One of the perks of being the boss, I suppose.

"He can squeeze you in more places at once than anyone I know, and sometimes you don't even notice," Molly Middleton grumbled to her fellow drudges in the ladies' toilet, the only place they could enjoy a Woodbine. For that was another of Randy Ronald's rules with which he had acquainted me at that first interview ... "I don't allow the staff to smoke. It stinks up the office." He had issued this *caveat* while lighting up and puffing at a King Edward cigar. No doubt another perk accorded only to top management, I thought.

Yes, those were heady days ... I enjoyed being Chief Accountant and enjoyed even more the kudos of the Ford Cortina that came with the job; only senior staff were allocated company cars and granted use of the executive canteen and executive toilets – wherein Randy Ronald had his own private partitioned-off cubicle – though it was not a good idea to follow him into this area as the man could give off odours that would challenge any deodorisers.

I remember well the first time I arrived home in the smart, new company car and parked it outside the house.

"Stuck up git!" Harry Wolstenholme had mocked as I got out on the driver's side. Harold was a good neighbour, but not exactly a friend.

"What would you do if I scratched the side of it?" asked his lad Jimmy, struggling to keep up with the long strides of his six-foot-tall father as they got nearer to me and the shiny Cortina. Jimmy was a good kid and I knew it was only a joke.

"Wouldn't half blunt the blade of your penknife," I told him.

It was all in good humour, but I knew I was the envy of the street, and lapped up every minute of it.

The rise in salary that came with the promotion meant we could, for the first time in our lives, afford a holiday abroad. Edna lost no time in gathering armfuls of brochures from every tour operator in the shopping precinct. No half measures with my missus ... "Colorado," she announced after scanning the small print on every page of every brochure. Once she had made up her mind there was no point resisting, so Colorado it was, later that year. Secure in the knowledge that a good pension also went along with the job, we enjoyed a few good holidays and hoped to enjoy a few more in our twilight years in the distant future. Then, wham, bang!

Here I am, sitting on a dry-stone wall trying to convince some other poor sod who has found himself surplus to accounting requirements, that redundancy need not be the end, but a new beginning ...

CHAPTER 2

Coffee, Two Sugars

"How did they break the news to you?" my companion on the dry-stone wall asked. "Were they kind or did they just not give a damn?"

* * * *

"Coffee, two sugars, biscuits, your favourite digestives," my secretary said, placing a tray before me. Only that morning in the shower I had noticed my spreading waistline and promised myself I would start a diet – and that was *before* Edna's uncomplimentary remark about my resemblance to Buddha.

I took a sip of the coffee and a bite of a digestive, vowing to start the diet tomorrow.

"Great Man wants a word," Ronald Higgins' secretary told me on the intercom. "Now – ten minutes ago – you know what he's like." She didn't wait for a reply but put the receiver down with a force that registered like a thunder-clap in my ear.

"Go straight in," she ordered when I reached her interconnecting office. She was looking at the nails she was filing and not at me. She had started her working life as a check-out girl at Kwiksave but since reaching her exalted position as secretary to the Managing Director of a toilet roll manufacturers, she tended to look down her long nose on us lesser mortals.

"Bet he's knocking her off," I overheard Irene Strangeways telling Molly Middleton as she closed the door to the ladies' toilets.
I approached Randy Ronald's door cautiously but, having worked damned hard on the company's behalf, I felt I had nothing to fear.

"Take a seat," he instructed, pointing to a chair with legs some two inches shorter than the leather one from which he could look down on his victims. Confident that he was about to discuss my annual pay increase, I was hoping as I sat down that he was in a generous mood. He sat behind a fog of King Edward's smoke.

"You'll have heard rumours no doubt that we are re-organising – introducing new blood, upgrading and down-loading so to speak." It was a statement and not a question so I didn't respond. But in my head I was picturing a seat on the Board and a swap of the Cortina for a BMW. He seemed to be waiting for some sort of response from me, so I nodded.

He sucked on his cigar.

"No point beating about the bush," he said. "I'm sorry, but I have to let you go."

Let me go? He sounded anything but sorry.

"If you'd like to clear out your desk and leave the car keys with my secretary, your redundancy money will be forwarded to you in the post. No point hanging on. Know it will be a bit of a shock ... we'll pay you to the end of the month of course."

Redundant? I sat there stunned. He stood up from his leather chair to encourage me to do the same. He came around the desk and extended his hand to shake mine.

"Regards to your wife – bring her to see us sometime." Before I reached the door I was, to him, a thing of the past. After years of loyal service, I no longer existed so far as he was concerned.

"I'll miss you," Molly Middleton sniffed, lifting the hem of her white overall and blowing loudly into it.

In the space of ten minutes I had developed a raging headache and indigestion. I made for my office to set about clearing out the drawers before departure.

"This my office?" The new young blood sat behind my desk. "Any chance of a coffee?" he addressed Hilda, my secretary, who had heard the news already via the grapevine and who was sniffing even louder than Molly Middleton

"He's a little shit," she said once New Blood was out of earshot.

"He's the boss's son," I told her, "so watch your back, me love, or you'll be next for the chop."

I recalled how Ronald Higgins had been delighted when his son had qualified as an accountant. He had introduced him to me at a Christmas do. The boy was very pleasant.

"You'll get to like him, Hilda," I assured her.

"Will I?" she said, registering her doubt.

"Redundant?" my wife screamed at the news. "I never did like that chap. Sneaky, snobbish, up himself ..."

She'd forgotten how she'd fawned and slobbered over him at the Christmas dance – she thought I never noticed that she didn't object when he stroked her bottom.

Hilda kept me up to date with the office gossip. She'd stop by once a month, discredit Randy Ronald for half an hour and then recount office affairs. And affairs there were ... seems New Blood had wasted no time in bedding Randy Ronald's secretary and putting her in the family way. Randy Ronald was not pleased – loving one's son did not extend to sharing favours with him. He was even less pleased when she insisted that his son should make an honest woman of her.

"Marry him? Over my dead body," he had roared at the time.

"Many a true word spoken in…" she had begun.

"What the hell do you mean?" he had screamed.

His secretary looked at her hand, running her thumb along her long, red-painted fingernails.

"Does your wife know about our little affair?" she threatened.

She married New Blood a month before the birth. Hilda said the baby was beautiful. She added though that the child bore a striking resemblance to the Chinese cook who worked in the canteen.

CHAPTER 3

I Fell in Lust

I noticed my companion on the dry-stone wall was nibbling at his sandwich now, a little more relaxed. "Go on," he urged. "How did you meet your wife?"

* * * *

I fell in love with her voice, soft and sexy. In the bar of the Dun Cow, Edna ordered two pints of bitter and four packets of Smith's crisps, salt and vinegar.

I also fell in love with her magnificent cleavage as she rested her ample upper portions on the bar top. I suppose it was the four pints of sparkling bitter that gave me the courage to ask her out.

Two months later in the romantic atmosphere of the Taj Mahal restaurant we were celebrating our anniversary – three months. I was just finishing off my prawn curry when I felt a tingling under my armpit. Her soft, sexy voice delivered the news most men would prefer not to hear …

"I'm pregnant," she said.
A prawn stuck in my throat.
"Don't joke," I told her.
"I'm not," she said. In the space of a minute her voice had lost all its sexiness, her bosom had lost all its appeal. The news instantly induced a headache and indigestion.

"Is he having a stroke?" the waiter asked anxiously. His words seemed far away and I seemed to be drifting through a fog. Must have happened the night we won the Darts and Crib

Trophy at the Workingmen's Club, I was thinking. I know I had a fair amount to drink that night and I know there was no machine in the Gents' toilets and it was too late to call at a chemist's.

On the way home Edna had dragged me into Asa Cook's barn and ravaged me, not entirely I might say against my will. I took her screams of ecstasy to be in appreciation of my sexual prowess. I was lying back in the hay congratulating myself on a job well done when a rat skipped over her foot and nearly induced a convulsion.

"You enjoyed that, love?" I asked expecting affirmation of my technique. "Did the mountains move for you?"
"Not really," she said, "I got cramp in me feet."

I loved Edna but marriage had not been high on my list of priorities. I wanted to travel before settling down. The last thing I'd expected was news that she was expecting! Perhaps, I thought, now might be the time to apply to the Merchant Navy.

But Edna's mother was ready with the shotgun.

"So when's the wedding?" she asked. "Don't expect me to be giving up me bingo to baby-sit. How the hell did it happen anyway?"

I wondered if I should tell her – every explicit detail.

"Did you hear that, Dad?" she addressed her unconcerned husband stretched out on the settee with the remote working overtime, flies gaping open displaying underpants that would not pass the bright light test, four empty lager cans and a half-eaten potted meat sandwich on the floor beside the settee. For a moment I thought he was crying, but then I noticed the smoke from his Woodbine was making his eyes water. He was not an inspiring picture by any standards. Mick, his greyhound, curled up on the fireside chair, cut a prettier dash.

"Did you hear?" his wife bellowed. "Your daughter is pregnant."

"Oh yes," he said mustering a little bit of interest, "and how did that happen? Oh hang on – University Challenge – my favourite programme. Talk to me later about it, eh?"

He was totally unconcerned about the whole affair.

Edna's mother, who was not fond of animals and positively hated greyhounds, slapped the dog with the pot towel she was holding. It jumped off the chair, whining.

"Oy!" her husband yelled, "don't take it out on the dog."
"It stinks," she said, still flapping at the dog with her pot towel.

The last sounds I heard that night as Edna and I departed the house were the dog yelping, her mother screaming and her father telling her mother in no uncertain terms to belt up.

The quick ceremony at the Registry Office was followed by a pint and a beef butty at the Dun Cow and then an hour's drive to the honeymoon venue in Blackpool. Two days at the Ravenous Crow down a street at the back of the Tower left me knackered. At three in the morning on the third day I lay back after a fourth session listening, gratefully, to her contented snoring. After an hour's respite she was at it again, nibbling my ear and stroking the inside of my thigh.

"Not again, love." I implored, but Edna showed no mercy.

"You don't have to worry, love," she whispered in my ear. "I'm not pregnant. I only said I was so that my mam would make us get married. I'll tell her when we get back that it was a false alarm."

This time I really felt like I was having a stroke. Those few words destroyed my trust in women for ever.

CHAPTER 4

Living with Redundancy

"I don't think I'll ever by able to adjust to being redundant," my companion on the dry-stone wall mumbled miserably. "Course you will," I told him. "It's only a question of mind over matter."

* * * *

To relieve boredom I set about doing all those jobs at the bungalow that Edna had been nagging about for ages and which I had shelved for one reason or another. I redecorated the whole place inside and out, I sorted out the garden shed, I oiled the lawnmower, I pointed the kitchen extension. Not only did these jobs keep boredom at bay, they also kept Edna at bay. Not being a woman accustomed to giving praise where praise was due (though she would argue this was because I never did anything worthy of praise), she actually told people that the garden was a credit to me.

But, unaccustomed as I was to such hard labour, this sudden exercise played havoc with my back.

"Lumbago. Take the pills and quit smoking," Dr Mac ordered.
"I don't smoke," I protested, but he wasn't listening as he scribbled away at his prescription pad.
"No lifting or bending," he ordered handing it to me and lighting up a Benson & Hedges before I reached the door.

So that was that – no lifting or bending – doctor's orders.

I discovered afternoon telly.

Countdown did wonders for me – I fell in love instantly with Carol Vorderman. Little men on horseback became familiar to me: Lord Oaksey smiled at me from the small screen in the corner: I came to regard Lester Piggot as a friend. But this new-found obsession nearly put me in the poor house. The bookie was always pleased to see me, counting his income from my losing bets almost before the race was run. While my investments financed private school education for his children and holidays abroad for him and his wife, I learned, slowly but ever so surely, to ignore Lord Oaksey ... and my feelings towards Lester Piggot became anything but friendly.

"Sitting around on your arse won't get you a job," Edna moaned at me. "Get down the Job Centre and see what's what."

Her friends at the Methodist Chapel would have been shocked at her choice of words, bearing in mind her crusade to rid the world of bad language, smoking and drug abuse.

"I am trying," I protested.
"Well, try harder," she advised.
So off I went.

The youth at the Job Centre was sucking contentedly on his ball-point pen.

"What about a School Crossing Attendant?" he asked.
"Bollocks," I replied. The ball-point shot across the room. His assistant brought him a cup of coffee. I could have murdered one myself just then but she never offered. He smiled at the girl clad in Gucci white tailored trousers and Next cashmere sweater.

"Thank you, Myrtle," he smirked. Creep. I knew *his* game.

Reluctantly he turned back to me.

"Car park attendant then?" he suggested.

"Bollocks," I told him again.

Not only did another ball-point hurtle across the room but he spilled the freshly-delivered coffee down the front of his Paul Smith shirt.

"Shit!" he jumped up, irritated.

Myrtle was still within earshot. She turned and delivered a snooty look in the direction of the coffee-bedraggled youth, annoyed more at the fact that he had possibly ruined his chances with her than the fact that he was unable to find me suitable employment.

Edna was waiting with bated breath.

"Any luck?" she asked.
"Yes," I said. "I didn't get a job."
"I hope you don't think you've retired ..."

She'd been happy enough to accept the redundancy cheque the minute it arrived, but I had the feeling now that my being at home interfered with her daily routine, and when her friends from the Tuesday Club arrived for coffee and cakes she always suggested a long walk might do me good.

"You can't just keep sitting around," she kept telling me. "Take up a course in dry-stone walling, or join the golf club, or take up bowling – there's a club in the park..."
"I'm going to the dogs," I said, cutting off her list of suggestions in mid flow.
"It's time you packed in that silly game," she said. "I'm telling you – it's me or the dogs."

Dog racing is a sport that's always been close to my heart. Her threats heralded the demise of our marriage. If she was making me choose between her and the dogs, the dogs would win.

CHAPTER 5

I Head for the Open Road

My sandwich benefactor on the stone wall was becoming really interested. "So how come you stayed with her all those years?" he asked. "Habit, I guess," I said.

* * * *

I'd had a bad night at Belle Vue dog track. Lady Luck had ignored me completely. Edna, in one of her sulky moods, also ignored me when I arrived home.

Greyhound racing, as I've said before, is a sport dear to my heart. I am overwhelmed with tenderness when I see my four-footed friends, especially those I have backed, crossing the winning line.

But Edna never saw it that way. I don't think she should have expected me to give up my hobby just because I'd lost my wages that week on Trap 4. After all, I would never expect her to give up Chapel if she lost at the Tuesday Club's bingo session. I thought it was very unreasonable of her to suggest it and I told her so.

She was grunting her discordance as she put on her coat.

"Well, I'm off to 'The Wives' – there's a chap giving a talk tonight on how to come to terms with redundancy. I intend to ask him how to come to terms with being married to a gambler."

And with that she slammed the door behind her.

The smell of cooking chicken filtered through from the kitchen. I hate chicken, and she knew it.

I had a hundred quid left in my pocket – managed to save it from the dogs. I took my coat from behind the door. There was something final about the click of the lock.

When you've been on the road for a while, you begin to be thankful for small mercies. Myself, – after spending nights in a derelict barn on Saddleworth Moor – I'm grateful to architects and designers of shopping malls, they offer the luxury of warmth and shelter and there is always somewhere to sit to watch the world go by. Shopping precincts smell clean and of scented polish – derelict barns on Saddleworth Moor do not.

It had been some time since I had been back in town. A wagon driver on his way from making deliveries in Halifax had offered me a lift. He was a kind chap ... didn't ask too many questions. He dropped me off at the end of the by-pass.

God, was I surprised at the changes! Roads were wider, shops were bigger, the new shopping mall hadn't even been built when I was last around.

I'd been sitting one day for quite a while, waiting for the warmth to get through the layers before venturing back out into the open, when a security guard eyed me suspiciously:

"Uh-oh," I thought as he approached me, "about to be pitched out again." To my surprise he bent down and slipped me a quid.

"Get yourself a coffee," he said, looking embarrassed. I made for the coffee shop inside the mall, gripping the one-pound coin gratefully. The woman who approached the table was around fifty, her long nose having difficulty balancing her spectacles. She stared at me somewhat disdainfully. I stared right back.

"I can pay," I said, showing her the one-pound coin.

"Oh," she said, a little flustered. "I was going to ask you something, but then it's rather personal, and perhaps ..."

"Ask away," I said.

"Well," she began, "I attend this Creative Writing class and my tutor suggested I get out amongst people to research the novel I'm writing."

Condescending old biddy, I thought.

"Perhaps," she cooed, "you would be so kind as to tell me how you came to this ... how you became a tramp?"

I sometimes indulged these busy-bodies by saying it was due to a failed love affair – women loved that angle – and sometimes I merely pretended to be deaf. – But this patronising old madam was getting on my wick.

"No, I will hell as tell you my private business," I told her. She looked taken aback.

"Might I ask why not?"

"Because it's none of your bloody business, that's why," I said. She scurried away, hiding her effrontery while searching the tiny cafe for signs of a more fruitful investigative interviewee.

She ignored the young couple at a table facing me.

"Bet he pongs," the pale, lank-haired youth remarked to his anaemic-looking girlfriend. Bet the only time they produce a few exotic colours is when they're thrashing about in passion, I thought.

"Looks like a good soaking in carbolic would do him no harm," she agreed, not bothering to lower her voice.

"He drinks. You can tell from looking at him," a huge bloke with a red nose and a faceful of broken veins joined in the communal criticising.

And you should know mate, I thought.
Now it was the turn of the two fat ladies at the table by the counter.

"Bet it's the likes of our husbands, May, who are keeping him in idleness," the one with a squint remarked.

"My Josh sez…" I looked up at the sound of this last voice. Unlike her friend, May had no squint but she did have a fat arse. So she married old Josh, eh? Her arse was nowhere near as big as that when I dumped her.

CHAPTER 6

Norman's Tale

"People are so unkind," my companion on the dry-stone wall commiserated. "They should be thinking 'there but for the grace of God go I' shouldn't they?" "Yes, life on the road can be tough," I agreed, "but nothing to life in prison, I expect."

* * * *

I decided it was time I visited Norman. Rumours had abounded for years about how he'd come to be banged up in Strangeways. I hitched a lift with a long-distance lorry driver who dropped me at the prison gates without asking any questions.

Norman was surprised and pleased to see me. He didn't get many visitors.

"You never did tell me how you wound up here," I said.

Norman laughed.

It seems that after a hard day at the mill – he'd been the foreman in the packing department – he had driven home in his Mini, battling against ferocious winds lashing sleet against the windscreen. At the junction of the by-pass leading to the motorway, a traffic policeman signalled to him to stop. Abandoned cars littered the road.

"You'll have to continue on foot," the white ghost instructed.

"On foot? That's impossible," Norman had told him.

"That's as may be, but it's the only way you'll get home tonight."

A sudden gust sent the constable's helmet flying up the motorway access road and he dashed after it, struggling to keep his feet against the force 6 gale that was ripping through his great coat. He soon disappeared from Norman's view into the white hell.

His wife was watching Coronation Street on television when Norman eventually arrived home. The wind whipped the door of the cottage from its hinges and he fell into the little porch, the wind continuing to beat up the world outside.

"Shut the bloody door, for God's sake!" she yelled, never taking her eyes off the screen. "If you want sommat to eat, warm up a tin of baked beans and there's some fish fingers. And I'll have a coffee too."

Well, you can imagine – "For God's sake, Mona. Baked beans and bloody fish fingers on a night like this!" Norman shouted.

Even before the storm had got up, it had not been one of Norman's better days. Flying Lydia, his favourite racing pigeon, had developed a bad case of dandruff. It might have been pneumonia, he was so upset about it.

As he was still investigating the contents of the kitchen cupboard – row upon row of tins ... pineapple chunks, tuna fish, mushy peas, fruit cocktail, soup, ham – ah, there they are, baked beans – he was wondering if Mona had heard reports that there was a world shortage of tin or sommat and she was apparently stocking up just in case it was true. He hoped it was that and not that she had become a kleptomaniac at Soopasavers up the road.

As the brass band of the 'Corrie' title music faded, she stood up, put on her coat and casually announced,

"Well, I'll be off then."

With a cursory peck on the cheek she departed without further explanation.

Norman toyed with the tin of baked beans. The idea was not at all appetising to him, so he decided he'd battle through the storm again to enjoy a pint and a pie at the pub. He rarely ventured into the Legion but it was nearer than his usual "local" and the sleet had turned to snow.

Possibly owing to the weather (though that would never be enough to put off the likes of Norman) the bar was almost deserted, save for a group of people in the corner laughing raucously.

A woman was dancing in the middle of the conclave and with each turn she displayed red garters around her ample thighs. The glass she waved in punctuation contained her favourite tipple – gin and tonic. Her small but appreciative audience, tapped her bottom and pushed money into her cleavage as she danced. One man – balding, beer belly, grinning like a Cheshire cat – was paying her more attention than the others. Norman recognised him as the manager of Soopasavers. He recognised the dancer too. Mona was astonished at the sight of Norman fast approaching the little group. And putting two and two together, as you do, the mystery of the cupboard full of Soopasavers tins became clearer to him.

Mona gathered her skirts and her wits about her quickly and explained,

"We were discussing him giving me a job."
"And is that all he is giving you?" her husband enquired vehemently.

The manager of Soopasavers shot to his feet.

"I really must be off," he addressed the group hoping to make a quick exit before the conversation developed into blows. "We can discuss the possibility of your joining Soopasavers another time, Mona. Nice to meet you, Mr. er... Mona. Must dash. I promised a friend to help him out – he's manager of the Erotica Gay Bar in town. Do you know it, err...Mr er...? Well, no, I suppose not."

And he scampered to the door clutching a white silk scarf that would offer no protection at all against the icy blast outside.

"Huh," Norman scoffed in a loud voice. "Swings both ways, does he?"

He took Mona's coat from the back of the chair, flung it at her and bellowed,

"Cover yersell up, woman. Who d'ya think you are? Bloody Sam Fox?"

There was little dialogue on the way home – Norman thought if she spoke he would finish up clocking her one and Mona knew better than to open her mouth.

Once home she opened a tin of baked beans in silence, emptied them into a Pyrex dish and popped them in the microwave. She put four fish fingers under the grill and took a plate from the rack. Ten minutes later she delivered the supper to her husband, sitting at the table knife in one hand fork in the other standing on end and tapping them impatiently. He took one forkful of baked beans and opened his mouth to complain, but in the event he didn't get the chance.

"I'm leaving you," Mona announced matter-of-factly.

His mouthful of beans shot across the table.

"You're what?" he shouted.

She had let this little titbit drop as if she had only just thought about it. Norman, who already had his suspicions, considered them confirmed now. The quantity of Soopasaver tins in the cupboard left no doubt.

Mona had started mopping up the spilled baked beans, but then thought better of it.

"I met him at the flower arranging class at the Legion on Tuesday afternoons. Tuesday's his afternoon off from the supermarket."

Norman was gobsmacked. How dare she suggest she was leaving him? If anyone was going to leave anyone, it was going to be him – leaving her!

She undid the tapes at the back of her apron.

"I've already packed. I'll stay at the Dun Cow tonight and collect the rest of my things tomorrow."

Somewhat unconvincingly she added,
"I'm sorry, Norman."

So when Hilda Duckworth from next door told him that the Soopasaver's manager's car was often parked outside the house at lunchtime it came as no surprise to him.

"Helping you out," Hilda Duckworth had smirked. "That's what he said, helping you out." At this point Norman was seriously considering crushing the manager's nuts. But then he had a better idea. Crushing his nuts would offer only temporary appeasement ... revenge of a more conclusive nature would be more satisfying.

Norman thought about his pigeons. He'd call Jack at the Three Feathers – he was the only person he could ever trust with his prize-winning birds. Jack had told him when he was presented as Breeder of the Year at the Annual Pigeon Fanciers Award Ceremony that if ever he wanted to sell, he would be willing to buy. But no, Norman decided he would give the pigeons to Jack.

He formulated his plans and began to put them into action.

Norman was packing into cardboard boxes everything that belonged to his feathered friends ready for handing over to Jack when a knock at the door interrupted him.

There, twitching and shivering on the doorstep was the Soopasaver's manager. After some stuttering from him and silence from Norman, unless a stone-faced stare of thunder counts, he stammered,
"I've come for the rest of Mona's things. We're leaving tonight together. I do love her, Mr er…, er…"

Norman motioned to him to step inside and the Soopasaver's manager dutifully obeyed, following Norman into the lounge.

"You see," he began to explain pathetically to the cuckolded Norman, "my wife doesn't understand me."

Norman surveyed the pitiful, trembling mass that was the Soopasaver manager. He was almost tempted to think twice about his plan, but then he reached under the table for the shotgun he had strategically placed there in readiness. As he raised the barrel towards the face of this shivering excuse for a man, the left eye of the Soopasaver's manager began to twitch and then developed into a full-blown spasm, beads of sweat dripping from his nose. For a moment there was silence – Norman levelled the gun and the Soopasaver's manager twitched.

Norman sensed his passion for Mona was rapidly evaporating.

"No, please, no," he whined. "You can have her back. I'll tell her it's all over. I'll never see her again."

That's true, Norman thought.

The blast from the shotgun lifted the Soopasaver manager off his feet and sent his dentures flying across the room. Blood was splattered onto the wall but by now Norman was not concerned about any redecorating that would need to be done.

Mr Soopasaver lay stretched full length on the floor. His left eye had stopped twitching but his right eye shuddered a bit and then, instead of his eyes closing like they do in the gangster films, both eyes remained open to stare at Norman. The carpet was soaking up the blood oozing from the area of his chest. A stain formed at his crotch.

And Norman could imagine St Peter saying, "Was it worth it Mr Soopasaver?"

Norman picked up the telephone and dialled the Police Station. 'Course he did have a licence for the gun – it had been a present from Snodgrass's widow after Snodgrass had accidentally shot himself while poaching on the estate where he was officially the game-keeper.

"Hang on, hang on," PC Hargreaves said. "I'll be round in a tick and you can fill me in." Norman sat down to await the knock on the door.

"Good God!" PC Hargreaves said, studying the late Mr Soopasaver laid out on the floor with eyes still open and still oozing blood.
"Did you have to shoot him today? Only it's the wife's birthday and she's expecting me taking her out for an Indian."

That's right – get your priorities right, Norman said to himself, picturing gallows and Pierrepoint waiting in a black mask.

The trial didn't last long. It was a cut and dried affair. Norman pleaded guilty and got "life".

He didn't miss Mona at all but he missed his pigeons and the club. So much for the Birdman of Alcatraz rubbish, he thought – they said that film was true but they wouldn't let him have his pigeons behind the bars of Strangeways Prison.

Norman was playing table tennis one day – two games up at the time – when one of the warders approached him with a pink envelope in his hand.

"Letter for you," he said.

To Norman's surprise it was from Mona asking if it would be all right for her to visit – 'I still love you' she had written and then three neat little crosses.

"Why not?" Norman decided.

So it was that a week later Mona arrived in her best Chapel clothes and smelling of *Coty L'Aimant*. Norman almost fancied her again, but not enough to apply for a conjugal rights visit – though she was after all still his wife. She flung herself upon Norman, kissing, cuddling, whispering. The warders turned a blind eye, for Norman was serving life and there were few privileges he enjoyed.

"I'll wait for you, Norman," Mona was whispering.
"Life's a long time," Norman pointed out.

It was not at all obvious that he was behind bars for the murder of her boyfriend.

"However long it is, I'll wait," she assured him.
"Good," he said. "I'd hate you to pop your clogs before I've had chance to shoot you too."

This was not the response Mona was expecting. She fled.

Norman continued to serve his time without moaning. He hated the slop bucket and the all-pervading stench of urine that was ever present but he never moaned.

Each night at lights out he would wish he could have a couple of birds in his cell ... the feathered type or the unfeathered type, he wouldn't mind which.

Jack at the Feathers wrote from time to time, reporting on the progress and achievements of his beloved pigeons, and then one day he reported also that Mona had emigrated to Canada with a young manager from the Food Emporium.

"Damn and blast," Norman said when he read that, and then he lay back on his bunk and in his mind he was boarding a Boeing with his shotgun.

CHAPTER 7

Two Bottles of Gold Top

"Course, it's not all fun and games being on the road, you know," I told my companion on the dry-stone wall. "There are good days and bad days. But unlike working in the toilet roll factory, there are more good days now than bad."

* * * *

It didn't start off with a feeling that it was to be my lucky day. I'd spent the cold night in a bus shelter on a hard, unforgiving form and was actually thinking to myself, "I'm getting too old for this lark."

Across the road from the shelter, a lady in pink fluffy slippers and pink dressing gown was taking in the milk from her doorstep – two bottles of Gold Top. I tormented myself with thoughts of a warm cup of milky coffee. As she straightened up, the lady in pink slippers caught sight of me emerging from the bus shelter.

"Do you fancy a cuppa?" she asked. There was nothing patronising about her tone, just warmth and kindness.

"I'd love one," I said, amazed that such a woman would welcome a tramp into her home let alone trust one.

She tucked one bottle under her arm and waved her free hand.

"Go round to the kitchen – the door's at the back."

As she opened the back door to let me into the kitchen, the smell of fried bacon and eggs oozed over me.

"Sit yourself down," she said, pushing the plate of food across the table to me.

"Isn't this yours?" I asked, trying to be polite though at the same time dying to get stuck into the bacon.

"It was, but I can soon make some more," she said.

She poured two cups of coffee and sat across the table from me sipping hers while I gobbled the food hungrily.

"I expect you could use some clean, dry clothes," she said suddenly, then added quickly, "oh, please don't take offence. My husband passed over a month ago ... he fell off the ladder decorating the ceiling ... I packed up his clothes to give to Oxfam but haven't been into town since."

She stood up from the table and beckoned to me to follow her into the lounge. She spread a newspaper on a chair and motioned to me to sit.

"Look what a mess he's left me in," she said. "A half decorated room. He was inconsiderate even to the last. I'll have to get someone in to finish the place. Not only that, he nearly killed the cat when he fell off the ladder."

For one frightening moment I thought she was about to ask me to sort out her decorating, but she simply said,

"I tell you what – you go up and get into a warm bath and I'll get a few things ready for you before you go back on your travels." She pushed a clean, fluffy towel into my hand.

"Off you go," she said, shooing me like a naughty boy towards the stairs.

I departed clad in two pairs of her late husband's trousers, two thick jumpers, two pairs of socks and another two pairs in a rucksack, a pure wool overcoat, and a pack of sandwiches.

If there are angels amongst us, she most surely was one. She had given freely without asking for anything in return, not even a thank you. But I did thank her, and still do, every day that I'm on the road.

CHAPTER 8

Those Were the (Dog) Days

A dog bounded over the dry-stone wall on which I and my companion were sitting. The little Jack Russell leapt between the two of us, not stopping in its pursuit of some shadowy object moving quickly along the bottom of the wall at the other side of the field.

"Must have better eyes than we have," my companion said. "Either that or it's as hungry as I was before you arrived."

* * * *

I shaded my eyes. The sun was bright. Its warmth eased old aches. I breathed in deeply, savouring the delicious smell of new-mown hay. To feel the sun on your face, to smell newly-cut grass, to hear crows quarrelling, to watch ants working – what more could anyone want?

A couple of dogs bounded up to me, dissipating my reverie. Their owner hurried across, gathered in the two greyhounds and made his apologies for their rude interruption. The sight of the greyhounds brought back memories – memories of another life a long time ago. Till then I hadn't realised I missed the greyhound racing and the gambling habit that had precipitated the end of my marriage.

I remember bringing Yappy home.

"He's a sure winner," the bloke told me, "bred-in-the-purple. It breaks me heart to part with him, but me wife's poorly and I need to spend more time with her. And this greyhound takes up too much of my time."

I was always a sucker for a sob story. I'd heard many an excuse for getting rid of greyhounds once they were past their best, but he seemed sincere so I handed over the fifty quid. I never set eyes on him again.

I warned the dog on the way home of the reaction we would both get from Edna – "Yappy", I said, "her bark's worse than her bite" – but at the same time I was preparing myself for the explosion of all time when she saw him, bred in the purple or not. She had always made it quite clear what she thought of dogs, particularly greyhounds, but her reaction left me speechless.

"He's beautiful!" she declared, kneeling on all fours and hugging and kissing the confused animal. Yappy tried his best to indicate his need to go outdoors to perform an act of nature, but Edna would not let go. With Edna still hanging around his neck, he cocked one hind leg up and casually squirted on her skirt which was spread out on the floor where she knelt.

To my amazement, Edna still did not lose her temper.

"Naughty boy," she cooed at the dog, "peeing over mummy's skirt."

You could have knocked me down with one of Norman's pigeon's feathers. It was love at first sight. The dog could do no wrong.

Despite the fact that Yappy never won a race nor even ever managed to finish one, Edna loved him unconditionally.

I began to resent the animal. My wife showered more attention on it than she did on me; it ate best steak while I ate sausages; it snored on the rug in front of the gas fire when I was turned out in the rain to go collecting pools money to finance his excursions to the race track.

Then I had a brainwave. Well, actually it was Edna who unwittingly inspired the brainwave.

"I want a pet," she announced, expecting her wish to be my command.
"You've got one," I reminded her, "Yappy."
"I want a Staffordshire bull terrier," she insisted.

Now Edna, as I've said, was not fond of animals, with the exception of our bred-in-the-purple greyhound of course, so what the hell did she want with a bull terrier? However, mine was not to question why.

"Your wish is my command, dear," I said, departing for the pub.

This could just be the thing, I imagined in my naivety, to restore a degree of normality to the household. Yappy was more than a little interested in the opposite sex, so if I chose an amenable little bitch, the two dogs would become companions and Edna would be left out in the cold. She'd soon get fed up with being ignored and would beg me to get rid of the pair of 'em.

Well, that was the theory behind my thinking at the time.

Molly Riddle had a cross bull terrier – crossed with a donkey from the look of it. I knew she was looking for a good home for its recent litter of pups, and I knew her husband, Jimmy, would be in the pub.

"Take my word for it," he advised me, "let the buggers alone. They're vicious. Mind you, it never seems to attack the missus – it's allus me it goes fer."

Jimmy had had a few too many in the pub one night and in his inebriated condition had allowed himself to be persuaded to buy a puppy from a punter at the bar. It was a dear little thing, podgy and cuddly and he was sure that Molly would be so delighted that he would thus escape a lashing of her tongue for the late hour of his arrival home.

"I've got you a pet, my darling," he soft-soaped her, producing from under his coat the adorable little pup.

Molly was thrilled. She was so busy cuddling the thing and arranging some hastily put-together accommodation for it in a grocery box and Jimmy's old jumpers that Jimmy was able to creep up the stairs unscathed.

Over the next few days the dog sniffed around exploring its new home. It quickly chose sides. In no time at all it learned how to intimidate Jimmy, pinch his supper, snap at his heels.

The puppy, as puppies do, did not stay little for very long. Molly adored it and it adored Molly. But Jimmy could not stand it and it could not stand Jimmy.

Very soon he was on first-name terms with the staff nurse at work. She in turn became very familiar with Jimmy's anatomy. She knew every wrinkle and crease in his backside, every hair on his legs, every bone in his ankles – all the places where the dog regularly sank its teeth for pleasure.

"I tell you," he told me, leaning on the bar in the pub, "you'll regret it."

But Edna wanted a dog.

"Best thing to do then," Jimmy advised, "is to go and see Cyril Bottomley up at Highview – he breeds bull terriers. Mebbe a thoroughbred would have more refined habits."

I took his advice. Next day I made my way to number thirty, Birch Close, Highview Council Estate, overlooking the skin and hide factory.

It was almost three in the afternoon and I could hear Cyril Bottomley's missus, Eva, bellowing at him as if she was still in the weaving shed and competing with the racket of the looms.

"Get that bloody dog shit cleared up or yer out, dogs an' all!" She had a way with words did Eva.
"Owd Fanny Heptonstall's complained about the stink and racket again, sez she's reporting you to the RSPCA." I could hear Cyril Bottomley trying to get a word in edgeways.
"All right, all right," Eva began again, "so she is a nosy old bag and I know she's had it in for you ever since one of yours escaped and served that damned silly poodle of hers, but she does have a point – they do bloody stink!"
"Now hang on," Cyril felt he had to defend his canine pals, "the stink's from the skin and hide works, not from my dogs!"

Eva was not listening to him. She seldom did.

"Get 'em cleaned out," she repeated, "or else."
"Fair's fair, love," Cyril made one last attempt to protest ... "You know me back's been playing me up."

Eva had heard that one.

"Your back'd soon spring to life to get you to the pub," she started. "Get out of that bloody chair and sort 'em out." Then she heard my knock on the door. It was actually my third knock on the door – the first two had been overpowered by the strength of their argument.

"Oh, do come in," she smiled as sweetly as pie – do pies smile? – well, you know what I mean. Cyril eased his feet off the top of the gas fire. His dirty toenails jutted out from the holes in his sweaty socks, and with one foot he pushed a plate containing a rejected baked bean sandwich under the chair.

"'Scuse me if I don't get up," he muttered, "me back's bad."

Eva, with just a look, registered her indignation before departing to the kitchen.

"There's only one pup available for sale at the moment," Cyril said, "pick of the litter though, bred-in-the-purple."

Where had I heard that before, I thought? Cyril was rabbiting on, extolling the virtues of the pup's parentage, "...sired by The Duke of Abbeyville – her mother's Princess Stephanie of Heckmondwyke."

"Huh," Eva scoffed from the kitchen, "more like that bloody poodle of Fanny Heptonstall's."

I could see there was murder in Cyril's eyes at her divulgence of this snippet of information.

"Just gossip," he said to me quickly. "You know what women are like. As she's the last of the litter I could let you have her a bit cheaper."

That was good enough for me. I took the pup.

Just like Yappy, the pup's first reaction to Edna was to pee all over her skirt, I'm not sure whether in fear or excitement. She hugged the little pup to her – she never hugged me to her – and cooed over it,
"Well, did my little girl want to wee-wee then?"

And so Kate became one of the family. That's what Edna called her, Kate.

Yappy took to her immediately. The omens were looking good. My plan to restore the household to its former canine-free state was going along nicely.

All too soon the puppy began to imitate Yappy and adopt his habits. The adorable little puppy soon became a home-wrecker.

She first blotted her copy-book so to speak when the minister called on Edna to discuss Chapel matters; Kate was lying on her back at his feet awaiting his admiration.

"Isn't she sweet?" he said. As he bent to respond to her invitation to tickle her tummy, Kate promptly squirted up the sleeve of his jacket. He was anything but pleased, and Edna was not exactly overjoyed.

Kate's omnivorous appetite extended to plastic cables, slippers, and un-read newspapers, and she particularly favoured Edna's knickers.

Edna's best wool coat that she wore to Chapel presented a bit of a challenge to her but eventually Kate worked her way through the lining. I thought her days were numbered then, but Edna simply said,
"She's only a baby."
"And you'll never be an old lady if you carry on like this," I whispered to the dog. Her response was to squat down on the sheepskin rug. And it seems that even that was my fault.
"You've frightened her," Edna accused me to explain away this latest misdemeanour. We never did get it clean.

But her crowning achievement happened one night while I was watching 'Corrie' on the box. I nearly choked on my crisps when Edna's scream out-bellowed Vera Duckworth's on the telly.

Edna lay in a heap at the foot of the stairs. She had tripped on Kate who was sleeping at the top of the stairs. The gash in her head needed a dozen stitches, and her leg was in plaster for six weeks. But Kate, just like Yappy, could do no wrong.

"It wasn't her fault," Edna said.

A week after the accident, while Edna was still recovering, I offered to take the dogs for a walk.

"Won't be long," I told her.

I walked straight to the pub, the local market place for second-hand goods. My eyes scanned the lounge. I needed a stranger – a passing-through stranger who was unlikely to be passing this way again. I spotted my victim. A middle-aged, well-dressed man, leaning on the bar.

Kate could turn on the charm when she wanted. I ordered my pint and gently persuaded her (I yanked on the lead) to brush against the stranger's legs. He turned and looked down.

"That's a grand-looking animal you have there," he said.

"Hmm," I agreed. "She's a pedigree – bred-in-the-purple. Adorable thing. Pity I have to get rid of her. We're emigrating and I have to find her a new home."

As if Kate could hear my silent instructions, she sidled up against him again, then sat up and begged, and if dogs could smile I would swear she was smiling.

He was hooked.

"How much?" he asked. Little did he know I would have given the damned animal to him, but since he had asked,
"Fifty?" I said.

He handed me the money. I handed him the lead.

"Edna! Edna!" I shrieked as I returned home. "Edna, dearest, I don't know how to tell you."

Yappy jumped all over her and a chunk of plaster dropped off her pot leg.

"Where's Kate?" she asked anxiously.

"Oh, Edna," I forced myself to think of something really terrible, like losing a hundred quid at the dogs, so that genuine tears could come into my eyes. "Yappy set off after a cat. I couldn't hold on to his lead, you know how strong he is once he sets off ..."

"What, what ..." Edna pleaded with me to continue in spite of my obvious distress.

"Kate set off after Yappy, and the bus ... oh, Edna ... it wasn't the driver's fault ... the poor dog never stood a chance ..."

Edna jumped up forgetting her pot leg and bashing it against the sideboard.

"We must go to her," she said, to my alarm.

"No, no, dear," I had to think quickly here. "I couldn't face picking her up from the road. A lady on the bus got off and picked her up for me. She promised to give her a lovely burial."

I thought poor Yappy might be in for a bit of stick, since I had put the blame firmly on him, and oddly enough the dog was looking shame-faced as if he had something to fear.

"Oh Yappy," she said, cuddling him to her, "It wasn't your fault. Thank goodness we still have you."

Phew!

CHAPTER 9
Morris the Menace

"Did you say you had a Cortina?" my new friend on the dry-stone wall asked. "Hmm," I confirmed, tucking into the last of his sandwiches.

"Mine's a Ford. Parked up there. Expect they'll be taking it back, the firm. The girlfriend won't be too pleased. I don't suppose the wife will be over the moon about it either."

* * * *

My first car hadn't been a Cortina though. It had been a battered old Morris Minor – bought it for fifty quid, which was a lot of money in those days, and to those who have nowt I suppose it's still a lot of money. I pictured myself whizzing along country lanes, pulling the birds, saluting the AA man.

As I'd parted with my fifty quid to the bloke in the betting shop he had assured me that the little car had never let him down and was good for another few thousand miles or so.

"They don't make 'em like this any more," he had said, almost in tears at the parting. He stuffed my money into his pocket, and I never set eyes on him again.

There was one small thing I had overlooked. I couldn't drive.

There was one small thing the one careful previous owner had also overlooked – the car was not taxed or insured.

Still, home was only a short distance from the betting shop, so I decided to risk it on all three counts. After all, I'd been a passenger for years in other people's cars and I'd taken note of how they drove, so...

I confidently slid into the driver's seat. I fondled the steering wheel affectionately ... my own car, my very own car.

I checked the mirrors (no seat belts in those days), and signalled that I intended to pull out from the curb. I gently pressed my foot on the pedal, but without any further instruction from me the single-minded Morris Minor shot forward – straight into the path of a lady (I knew she was a lady because she cursed politely as her car slid along the side of Morris the Maniac, as I came to call him).

Without thought for the safety of herself or her vehicle, she parked in front of me, directly in the path of Morris the Menace whom I already distrusted to stay still. She got out of her car and approached, both hands on her hips and her Hush Puppies splashing through a puddle at the side of my car.

"If you intend to wipe out the population of this town," she said in a cultured voice, "then you are going about it the right way. Ah... aren't we lucky? Here is PC Hargreaves."

My heart sank.

"What have we here?" he asked bombastically.
"What we have here," Mrs Hush Puppies said, "is an idiot driver in an idiot car. Neither is fit to be on the road."
"Licence," PC Hargreaves said without moving his lips and holding out his hand to receive.

By now my teeth were chattering like the castanets of a Spanish flamenco dancer.

"I wasn't going anywhere," I lied. "I've just bought it and I was sitting waiting for my friend to drive me home (he has a licence) and I decided to turn the key and see if it would start up. I never touched anything and the damned thing just shot forward of its own accord."

"Hmm," said PC Hargreaves, obviously unconvinced. He turned to Mrs. Hush Puppies. "Well since no one's hurt, it's up to you, madam, whether you wish to pursue matters."

If there was one thing he hated it was filling in all those forms back at the station. No one had been hurt or it would have been a different tale.

Lucky for me the vicar pulled up on his bicycle behind Mrs Hush Puppies' car.

"Can I help?" he asked.
"Ah, vicar," I said. "I was waiting for you to drive me home. Can you confirm to this constable that you have a driving licence?"

Mrs Hush Puppies, who knew the vicar well and was obviously turned on by his dog collar, hastened to assure him.

"Well, there's really no need to take matters further," she said to PC Hargreaves while grinning at the vicar. "No real harm's done."

And they went their separate ways while the confused vicar sat in the driving seat of Morris the Menace awaiting an explanation.

"We'll soon have you driving," the young man at the driving school assured me. He flicked through the pages of his appointments diary, his long fingernails scanning the columns.
"Ah, Wednesday at three? How does that sound?"

His voice was high pitched and his aftershave overpowering. I had my suspicions but I'm not prejudiced.

Well that Wednesday at three *was* fine – and the next after, and the Wednesday after that, and the next three months of Wednesdays. After the first Wednesday's outing, the long-fingernailed young man left the driving school to pursue another career – well, that's what instructor number two told me. Instructor number two stuck it out for three Wednesdays before suffering mental and physical exhaustion and being ordered to take sick leave. Instructor number three was a woman – nuff said. Instructor number four said he didn't like Morris Minors. Instructor number five was determined to get me beyond the drawing-away-from-the-curb stage and he succeeded, though I later learned that he always fainted at the sight of Morris Minors after that. Instructor number six was made of sterner stuff. His perseverance paid off and the date of my driving test loomed ever nearer.

"You'll be okay," he assured me as I arrived on Doomsday, though I did notice his fingers were crossed as he said it.

My smile changed to a wince when I saw the driving examiner was none other than Mrs Hush Puppies. She did not smile back.

"Turn left here," she said.

God knows why I turned right.

I could feel my chances of passing slipping away even at this early stage of the test.

"Reverse into this space," she instructed.
"It's only the exhaust," I explained when there was a crunching sound of metal on curb. I got the feeling she was irritated by the way she was gritting her teeth and tapping her clipboard.
"When I tap the dashboard, apply your brakes to make an emergency stop," she commanded.

I did – perfectly I thought. As she bent forward to retrieve her dentures from the dash where they had rebounded from the windscreen, I could have sworn I heard her swear.

"I distinctly said 'when I tap the dashboard' not when I am going to wipe my nose," she cursed. And the fact that I had accidentally turned up a one-way street where the traffic was facing me was absolutely no excuse for bad language.

Other road users were no more helpful. Anyone can make a mistake, or two, or three ...

One woman bawled at me to "Get out!"

"Some folk think they own the road," I said to Mrs Hush Puppies who, I noticed with some concern, had abandoned her clipboard and was clutching the sides of her seat with white-knuckled hands.
"She does," she said sarcastically. "You are in her private driveway."

The remaining length of exhaust fell onto the drive with a clatter after collision with a garden gnome. The woman was waving belligerently and questioning the marital status of my parents as Morris the Menace rejoined the public highway.

The rest of the test was uneventful, apart from Mrs Hush Puppies telling me I was doing fifty in a built-up area.

The finishing line came into view. It's questionable which of us was the more relieved. A Jaguar had parked in the spot I had vacated half an hour ago by the curb outside the Examination Centre, so the oncoming Juggernaut forced me to complete my journey on the pavement.

"The examiner just didn't like me," I said in an effort to explain my failure when I got home.

CHAPTER 10

Where are they now?

"Shouldn't you be getting home?" I asked my companion on the wall. "Won't your wife be wondering where you are?" "Let her wonder for a bit," he said. I suspected it was the first time he'd had a smile on his face for weeks.

"That's the spirit," I told him.

We sat there quietly for a minute, both of us reflecting, but reflecting on different things.

"Do you ever wonder what happened to people you knew in your youth?" he asked at last. "Do you wonder if they are still in good jobs, living in security?"

It was 1942 when I finished my stint in book-keeping at Commercial College. That little piece of paper saying I was proficient in commercial studies was to be my passport to the world. I was ready for the challenge, and my first stop was the public library where I sat scanning the *Sits.Vac.* columns for a firm canny enough to want to employ me.

To one enthusiastic about conquering the world, the listed vacancies did not offer much scope ... "Trainee accountant required for small firm of clothing manufacturers" – "Young school leaver with Certificate in Book-keeping needed for busy commercial office". But then one caught my eye ... "Major film company based in the Midlands requires office staff in all categories. No experience necessary as training will be given, but a knowledge of book-keeping would be an advantage."

I glanced furtively around the library hoping no-one was looking, then tore around the advertisement, pocketed it, and folded the newspaper back neatly.

It did not for one moment enter my head that my application would be turned down. I wrote off in my neatest handwriting and fed the envelope into the mouth of the pillar box at the end of the street with every confidence. Though my parents were astonished, I was not in the least surprised to receive, almost by return of post, an invitation to attend for interview.

Printed on the envelope were the impressive words "Twentieth Century Fox".

"Off to be a film star then, are we?" the postman said sarcastically as I took the envelope from him.

First interviews were to be conducted at the office of the Branch Manager in Manchester and I turned up in my best bib and tucker two minutes early.

"Go straight in," the young girl on the reception desk instructed me, waving to a door marked "General Manager."

My first assumption, on opening the door, that the office was on fire was dismissed when a voice bellowed from inside a cloud of cigar smoke,
"Sit down, lad."

He pointed with his cigar to a leather chair directly opposite to him.

"Now tell me, have you seen *How Green was my Valley*?"

He started to cough. He spluttered and mopped his brow with a handkerchief in the same hand as the still lighted cigar. I waited for him to regain control ...

"Saw it last week," I lied. "Loved it." A bit of creeping never does any harm.

Taking into account many stops and starts for coughs and splutters, the interview lasted about half an hour. I agreed with everything he said – and even offered him a glass of water. I knew he was impressed.

And in the fullness of time, sure enough, the job offer arrived. I was to be posted at Head Office in Moreton Pinkney Manor in Warwickshire, as trainee book-keeper.

It was with a little trepidation that I packed my cases, for I had never been away from home before – unless you count the odd day trip to Blackpool, but then I'd always returned to sleep in my own bed.

"You'll be all right, son," Dad encouraged me. "Just keep your nose clean and there could be loads of opportunities for advancement in a company that size."

Mam stood sniffing on the doorstep.

"Take care," she was telling me as I hopped on the bus with my case. "Have you got your train ticket? Remember to eat well. Write as soon as you get there."

On that morning in September, 1942 the railway platform was crowded with people saying their tearful goodbyes – soldiers, sailors, airmen, ATS, WAAFs, Land Army girls – many of them I supposed like myself apprehensive at leaving home for the first time – bit excited too.

Three hours later I reached my destination. A black limousine was waiting for me and the chauffeur ushered me into the black leather back seat.

"'Bout three miles," he told me, "sit back and enjoy the ride."

This young scrap from the North had arrived. The lanes were lined with hedges beyond which I could see nothing but meadows and green grass – a far cry from the grime of the North. As we passed through a village I noticed the different colours of brick and stone that were not ingrained with soot and weather but were bright and clean. There was about this alien countryside a mesmerising sparkle so foreign to my eyes that at first it was hard to take it in.

Two stone lions guarded the entrance to Moreton Pinkney Manor. The grandeur of the place took my breath away. The chauffeur practically skipped up the stone steps, and opened the oak door while simultaneously calling, "It's only us." The informality of the announcement of my arrival seemed totally out of keeping with the splendour of the Manor. I'd expected a butler at least!

In the coming months I would mingle with the stars – Stewart Grainger, Margaret Lockwood, Clark Gable, Jack Warner, Florence Desmond – and movie moguls who today would be considered captains of industry.

I was thrown in at the deep end immediately – seconded to the accountant and answerable only to him. He was a decent chap and took me under his wing. My certificate of proficiency in book-keeping had served to get me the job, but in practice it was of little use ... just like learning to drive a car to pass the driving test but then once the L-plates have gone, learning to drive on the roads.

I wrote home often with tales of fraternising with the stars. Mam had always had a thing about Tyrone Power so I asked him for his autograph and sent it to her. She was thrilled to bits. I told my folks of the countryside – the thatched cottages, the fields with green grass in the spring and yellow hay in the summer, of sunlight sparkling in the morning through cobwebs heavy with dew on the hedges, of birds and flowers I did not recognise, and of the funny accents in people's speech that, unwittingly, I was acquiring myself.

It all seemed a far cry from the North of England I had left behind, and I wondered if I would ever want to return there. I did not of course mention these feelings in letters home, for I knew Mam would have been sad thinking I would never return.

On leave, I travelled up North for the odd weekend, but I was always glad to return to this haven in the Midlands, particularly in the spring when the hawthorn was heavy with white blossom and the coltsfoot nodded their yellow heads in the grass verges.

The hours were long and irregular – anything but a nine to five job. But I loved it, and because I respected the man I worked for, I worked hard to repay his confidence in me.

It wasn't all work and no play however. On Friday nights the Company opened up the Big Hall at the Manor and invited in the locals – mostly farmers and farm labourers and Land Army girls. Those Friday nights were social occasions when any airs and graces were dropped – stars danced with make-up girls and typists, and the villagers chatted to cameramen and accountants. I concentrated my wooing efforts on the Land Army girls – and was never disappointed.

It was a wonderful era in my life.

It was a sad day for me indeed when the Company disbanded and returned to its roots in the USA. Many of the senior staff went with them, but I was still a junior cog in a huge wheel and there were many others to recruit from – without having the expense of taking the likes of me with them.

For a long time afterwards, whenever I watched old films on television I would see in the list of credits at the end the names of people I had known – not just the stars but the camera crew and gaffers and lighting people, who had been my family and friends over those formative years in my life.

And, yes, I would wonder "where are they now?"

CHAPTER 11

Don't Pity Me

My companion on the dry-stone wall departed but not before he had surprised me. "Will you be here again, tomorrow?" he asked.

"Dunno," I said truthfully. "Depends on a lot of things."
"Like what?" he asked.
"Well, whether it's good walking weather, whether I die of pneumonia in the night."
"I'll tell the wife there wasn't enough lunch in that box today, so she'll pack twice as much tomorrow, then we can share it here. Okay?" he asked, almost pleading.
"Maybe," I said, but he knew I'd be there. I could never resist an audience for my tales.

* * * *

God knows why people pity me but some do. Those that don't just think I'm a dirty old bugger. I don't conform, you see. They spend their lives sitting in traffic jams breathing in exhaust fumes from the car in front. They live from one pay day to the next hoping there will actually be another pay day; they lumber themselves with mortgages, overdrafts, loans – and then they wonder why the doctor prescribes *Prozac*.

And the odd thing is that they consider themselves to be successful. Well, if that's the measure of success they are most welcome to it.

How many can say they have wandered freely over the purple heather of Scotland, have sat on the banks of Loch Maree watching the sun setting without a thought for where they will be spending the night? How many have soaked up the magic of Glencoe without worrying what time they were due to return home? How many have trodden the Pennine Way without a thought of what the family were up to? And how many have discovered the timeless tranquillity of the Cotswolds, stopping whenever the fancy took them to dangle their feet in the cooling streams and rivers? The Tyne, the Ribble, the Avon, the Severn, the Fowey – I've dangled my feet in them all.

The Pennines, the Chilterns, Dartmoor – I've battled through their snows and basked in their suns.

Yes, they can stuff their pity. I'm rich.

It's not been all sunshine and flowers though, I must admit.

I could see a storm brewing over the Snake Pass one afternoon so decided to seek shelter for the night a bit earlier than I'd usually take a halt on my travels. I could just make out the shape of some sort of barn to the edge of a field, so I set off to investigate. It was a derelict hen-hutch. It seemed like a good idea at the time – smelly, but dry and warm.

As the storm drew nearer, my accommodation grew smellier, damper and colder. By the time the full blast of the blizzard hit, my feet were numb, my hands were blue, and any brass monkeys around would have been panicking. I thought if I went to sleep I would never wake up. It would be years before anyone would discover my body – a heap of bones and rags. But it wasn't hard to stay awake – the noise was deafening with the wind shaking and rattling the old timbers and insisting on getting through every crack in that place.

To my own amazement I survived the night ... only to be chased by a bull as I was completing my ablutions in the snow. I ran faster than I had ever run in my life, but that was not fast enough. Suddenly I was floating through the air and if I hadn't landed on the other side of the wall I might have suffered another painful launching.

"Hey you!" a woman screamed at me, "what do you think you're doing on our land. Get off with yer! Yer frightening Eric."

So anxious was I to get off that I never felt the pain of Eric's intrusion. Once I reached the road and could be sure I was well out of Eric's range, as well as his irate owner's view, I sat down to recover on the first dry-stone wall I came to. And then I felt it. By hell, did I feel it.

My arse was sore for a month. In the end I dropped into the Casualty Department of the local hospital. The nurse's words were music to my ears.

"Drop your trousers," she said.

I've not lost that old magic then, I thought.

Have you ever had a tetanus jab? It was worse than the bloody bull.

Then there was the time I was casually walking across a field on the outskirts of Banbury. I was knee-deep in ragwort and hedge parsley, ducking out of range of the lapwings using me for target practice. Little did I know others might soon be using me for the same purpose.

"Get out of there, you silly old bugger," a bloke in uniform bawled at me. Somehow I'd wandered into an RAF practice bombing area. I tell you, I cleared that fence in double quick time.

But on the whole, I'd rather be "unsuccessful" and travelling the road than "successful" and sitting in traffic jams.

CHAPTER 12

Frank's Tale

By noon the sun had warmed up the stone of the dry-stone wall. I'd had a pint of milk on my way there – a milkman had spotted me in the bus shelter in the wee small hours and had handed me a bottle from his van. That was one thing I never did – I didn't steal. I was just about to give up on the redundant accountant when his car appeared. True to his word, he had brought more than enough lunch for two.

"Now where were we?" he asked.

I didn't need prompting twice.

"I was in Cornwall ..." I began.

* * * *

It was spring, I remember that.

Spring in Cornwall is like summer in the Pennines. Down there the crocus and daffodils had finished, in the Pennines they were hardly breaking through the top soil. There were flowers down there that I didn't even recognise.

I was passing a boat yard which, although it was early in the morning, was alive with activity.

"If you've got a day or two, I could do with some help," a bloke in sawn-off blue jeans and ragged cotton T-shirt said to me as I sat on a wall watching. "I'll pay you of course."

The money wasn't part of the equation.

"Glad to," I said.

I spent three weeks in Cornwall, helping him. He let me sleep in an old shed at the back of the boat yard. I could come and go as I pleased, and there was always a packed meal waiting there for me.

They were a retired couple, living on his pension, and spending most of it on this fishing boat that had seen better days. Luckily his wife approved of his hobby (unlike Edna who had strongly disapproved of mine) and welcomed the small remuneration that his fishing trips brought in.

I especially enjoyed the early mornings, the screeching seagulls were my alarm clock. I worked hard and enjoyed it, and my new friend trusted and appreciated me.

He took me out with him in the boat, the wind and spray from the sea leaving a salty deposit on my hands and face. I learned to clean out the fish, swill down decks, unload the catch, and any other job that needed doing. Though I didn't realise it at the time, I was so much a part of the boat and the sea that I was in danger of putting down roots and abandoning life on the road.

I began to envy this man and to resent the time I'd wasted in a stuffy office, never knowing even what the weather was like outside the dirty windows there. At the time I had thought I was lucky to have a job at all when so many people hadn't. But now, with the sun on my back and the wind in my face, I thought of the poor sods back there, rushing off to jobs they hated, worrying about mortgages, the rise in interest rates, redundancy always looming over their shoulders. Not to mention the dreaded, "I'm pregnant" from the wife.

Life does hand out some surprises though. I was having a glass of cider in the bar of The White Pony – the nearest pub to the boat yard – when Frank Beckworth walked in. He'd been Chief Wages Clerk at the Mill back in my accounting days.

"I'd heard you'd left home and taken to the road, but I thought it was just a rumour. I could imagine you leaving home for a woman, but not to be a ... er ..."
"You can say it, Frank. Tramp – that's what you mean, isn't it?"

He looked embarrassed but relieved. "Anyway, what about you?" I went on, "Heard you'd had your fair share of trouble. Did you leave the wife?"
"No, she left me. I arrived home from the Dun Cow one night and she'd left a note stuck to the television screen – 'I've left you' – I never met the bloke. He was a taxi driver. I silently thanked him. I sat back in the fireside chair listening to Suzanne Charlton telling me the weather was sunny and warm in Cornwall and cold and damp in Yorkshire."

He heaved himself up onto the bar stool beside me.

"So I thought to myself – Cornwall. That's what I thought. Why not? Now she's buggered off, I can do what the hell I like. I opened a Carlsberg and said 'Cornwall, here I come'. After a dozen more, I fell asleep in the chair – wouldn't have dared do that with her around, ha ha. Next day I closed up the bungalow and set off. I've been in love with this part of the world for years."

He was in full flow now. I ordered a couple more pints realising we were in for a long night. Frank was obviously glad to have a listening ear, so I listened as he related his tale of woe – oops, joy.

"It had taken me all day at the bungalow to pack stuff up in boxes and the bin was overflowing with her stuff. No point hanging on to things.

I departed by the light of a full moon. I must say I nearly had second thoughts at the sight of that there moon bathing our wonderful Pennines in silver, and the stone walls glistening in early frost and dew. Still, by daylight I'd reached the Devon border. The trees I'd left behind up there were still bare, not a leaf on 'em – but here they were not only in leaf but in blossom.

I stopped in Dawlish for a coffee at a cafe with gingham tablecloths. Even the waitress seemed more alive than those up theer (and here he nodded his head northerly).

Her accent when she spoke was warm and welcoming. The coffee was delicious. (He breathed in deeply as if he was savouring the flavour again).

It was lunchtime when I set off again. I made for the Fisherman's Rest in Pengarth where I knew the landlord after years of holidaying down here.

Harry was just opening up as I pulled into the car park.

"It's nice to see you," he said, "here on holiday again?"
"Not really," I explained. "Wife's left me." Harry fully understood I was not expecting sympathy.
"Thought I'd get right away and see if I am not too old to make a fresh start."
"Well," Harry said, "I could always do with some help in the pub. Won't be long now before the tourists start descending on us. We're actually full at the moment but I'm sure Jane'll find you a room over at her place."

I remembered Jane. The Fisherman's had won the skittles trophy and pints of amber nectar had flowed like a river in flood. Jane's husband, a nice chap, had enjoyed more than his customary three pints. The verdict was that he'd missed his footing on his circuitous route home and finished up in the harbour – his body never was found.

It was her lascivious curves, particularly those above the waist, that had first attracted me to Jane. She was plump, but then I like plump women. Long black hair swirled around her shoulders, and her smile filled the room with sunshine.

"Of course," said Jane when Harry asked if I could rent her spare room, which turned out to be conveniently across the landing from hers. (Here Frank gave a nod, nod, wink, wink, tapping his nose.)

I settled in immediately. I've got a job with the Council – just seasonal – street cleaning – but it's a long season down here. Then in the evenings I help out at the pub. Love it. But when I want a quiet pint, I come down here – somehow if I stay to drink at the Fishermen's I feel as if I should be working.

Jane's a great gal. Her husband never did appreciate how great.

Anyway, to cut a long story short, I decided to stay in Cornwall. I had to go back home to sort out affairs up there, but there was no doubt at all in my mind that Cornwall, with Jane, was where I wanted to live out my days.

To my amazement when I got to the bungalow my wife was there – on her hands and knees, scrubbing the kitchen floor, just as if nothing had happened.

"Oh, I wasn't expecting you," she smiled. "I gathered you'd have gone off to lick your wounds in Cornwall and would be back sooner or later, but not today. I was hoping to have the place spick and span before you returned. Don't know where you stacked all my stuff though. But never mind that, now. Would you like something to eat?"

I was flabbergasted.

I was even more flabbergasted when she sidled up to me, giving me that special look I hadn't seen in her eyes for many a long year.

"What happened to the taxi driver," I asked.
"Oh him," she said disdainfully. "Didn't tell me he had a wife and three kids."

She was wrapping her arms around me now, purring like a kitten.

"Hang on a bit," I started.
"Oh, Frank. I didn't realise what a treasure I had in you. I never stopped loving you, you know." Not even when you skipped it with the taxi driver? I was thinking.
"Do you think we can have another go – make a fresh start?"
"We can hell as like," I told her. "I've got an appointment with a solicitor tomorrow to sort out a divorce."

This time *her* flabber was gasted.

"You mean ...?"
"Yes, I mean," I told her, "go to hell."

CHAPTER 13

A Load of Old Cobblers

"See this wall we're sitting on?" I said to my companion, still enjoying the packed lunch his wife had provided for us. "Well I've built some of these in my time."

* * * *

I avoid towns whenever possible. I prefer the countryside. Sometimes food and shelter are easier to come by in a town, and sometimes needs must, but I always make my way back into the country as quickly as I can.

I was sitting one day on a dry-stone wall similar to this when I smelled the diesel of a tractor approaching.

"Want a couple of days' work?" Ted Giles called from high up on his exposed seat on the noisy tractor. "I could do with help rebuilding these walls and I'm buggered if I have the time or energy to face it on me own."

My experience of building stone walls was not extensive, but it turned out to be wider than his. The couple of days turned out to be a couple of weeks, but we finished before the bad weather set in.

"Do you fancy staying on a bit?" Ted Giles asked. "There's allus plenty to do on the farm and you'll have good shelter till the better weather comes."

I'd slept in the barn during the couple of weeks' wall-building and assumed I'd be sleeping there again. It was warm and dry and he was right about the bad weather on the way.

"Okay," I said.

"Hop on the back of the tractor then," he said and he set off towards the farm house.

Once in the cobbled yard, I jumped down from the tractor. My feet had hardly touched the ground when a dog bounded up snarling. It was quickly joined by two bad-tempered geese hissing.

"Tekk no notice of them," Ted Giles advised me, "their barks are worse than their bites."

But as if the still-snarling dog had heard, it brushed against my trembling legs, its great broad head on a level with my waist, casually cocked its hind leg and pissed down my trousers.

Ted Giles showed no concern at all.

"Got a guest for dinner," he announced making a grand gesture for me to enter the kitchen.

"Tekk your boots off the pair of you," was his wife's only comment.

"And *her* bark's worse than her bite too," Ted assured me.

"Hope yer not one of them veggies as objects to eating dead livestock," she said, ladling out delicious smelling lamb stew and making it fairly plain that if I were a vegetarian she would be offering no alternative.

I smiled and said, "Oh, that smells good," thinking that would be answer enough to her question, but she was obviously expecting rather more.

"No," I said. "I am happy to eat anything that's put before me, and grateful for it."

Ted sat down at the wooden table without washing his hands and grabbed a huge cob of home-baked bread, not buttered.

"Place is a bit of a shambles," he said through a mouthful. "Keep meaning to get it all sorted but it's too much for one and hers not much use at owt heavy."

The lamb stew in front of us was steaming. I politely waited for my hosts to begin theirs before I tucked into mine.

"I can't pay you much, but you'll have good food in you and warm shelter fer as long as you stays," he said.

And he was as good as his word.

I'd never fancied farming ... all that muck – mucking out, carting muck down to the midden at the bottom of the yard, spreading muck on the fields. Muck and more muck.

Ted and his wife didn't seem to notice the farm smells at all. I wondered if I would ever get used to it, but then I didn't intend to stay long enough to find out.

One day, the cows had just gone into the sheds for milking, and I was struggling with a barrow-load of foul-smelling dung across the cobbles in the yard. The cows *en route* had left their marks on the cobbles – shiny, smelly, wet marks. I slipped and landed head-first in the heap at the bottom of the yard.

Ted Giles came running when he heard my cries for help.

"Thought you'd done sommat serious," he said.

It was serious to me – lying in cow shit seemed bloody serious.

"Go on in," he said returning to the cow shed. "Wife'll find you some clean clothes. Keep this up and I'll have to visit Oxfam just to keep up with you." If he'd had a sense of humour I would have thought he was joking.

Mrs Giles (I never did find out her first name) looked at me in disgust.

"Here," she said, tossing a pair of trousers in my direction. "They'll fit. They were me dad's and yer about his size. They were his lucky pants he allus said. Mind you, he was wearing 'em when he fell through the barn roof and broke his neck. Still, can't blame a pair of trousers for that." She smiled, revealing a gap where two front teeth were missing from her upper set – did nothing for her appearance, the old girl.

Clad in my lucky trousers I headed for the cow shed to receive new orders.

"Pigs," Ted Giles said. "Tekk that bucket o' swill. Over theer look. Watch the owd sow, she can be a bad-tempered owd bugger."

The lucky trousers were anything but lucky. The latch on the gate to the piggery gave way and I slid into the enclosure, into the shit and into the bad-tempered old sow.

Ted Giles brayed like a donkey.

"This is getting to be a habit," he laughed, bending to pick up the now-empty bucket. But he was soon laughing on the other side of his face. There was a loud click and Ted was stuck, neither up nor down.

"Me bloody back," he screamed. "Get the missus."

Mrs. Giles and I soon got him into bed. When I left the house I could hear him banging on the floor with a stick, shouting "Where the hell are you woman!"

At dawn the next day I headed quietly down the lane, with my three-quid "wages" tucked into my boot.

No, farming is definitely not the life for me. That couple of months proved to me quite definitely that life on a farm is a load of old bullshit.

CHAPTER 14

Stud Farm – Help Wanted

My companion on the old dry-stone wall was looking decidedly more happy now. "Does the wife know yet?" I asked him. He shook his head. "Tell her tonight," I advised him. "Then if she doesn't like it, you can always join me on the road."

He smiled, though I knew he was not a survivor like me and the very idea of fending for himself in the open without knowing what was ahead would see him off. He was looking down at his feet, dangling from the wall, and beginning to let the depression seep into him again. So I quickly thought of a tale to cheer him.

* * * *

I could hardly believe my eyes when I saw the notice pinned to the farm gate – "Stud Farm – Help Wanted" – either this chap had a terrific sense of humour, or none at all.

But it was a woman who answered my knock on the door. She was in her forties, attractive, a cream sweater straining across her ample bosom and her jodhpurs anything but baggy around her thighs. She had a slight squint and though it made her face seem a bit lob-sided, she was in fact quite attractive.

"Do you know anything about horses?" she asked. The only horses I'd ever been interested in had little men on their backs, and I thought I might as well be honest.

"Huh," she scoffed. "No doubt those little men on horseback are the reason for your present predicament."

I didn't think that deserved a reply, so turned to walk away.

"Hang on there," she said. "Might as well give you a try. No-one else has applied and I need help."

She set off at a gallop across the yard. I wasn't sure if I was supposed to be following her, but then she turned and beckoned.

"Come on then, my man!"

In a corner of the barn was an old, cast iron bath tub served by two huge, old-fashioned, copper taps. She lifted a bucket out of the bath and plonked it on the floor of the barn.

"Clean yourself up," she ordered. "There's plenty of hot water – let it run a bit, it has to get from the house to here – then we'll discuss your duties over a meal – you look as if you could do with a good meal."

She departed the barn. I filled the tub, disrobed and put one foot tentatively in the water. The barn door rattled as it opened and I quickly shot below the water line. My modesty was not even noticed.

"Try these," she said flinging a pile of clothes onto a chair. There's a razor there. Get a shave while you're at it." Mrs Redrum was certainly used to giving orders. She gathered up the clothes I had discarded and threw a tablet of soap and a clean towel in my direction.

I lay for half an hour in that tub, breathing in the *Imperial Leather* and then using the badger-hair brush she'd left me to lather up my whiskers.

I pulled on the brown corduroy trousers – looked like new. I smelled the new socks before I tore off the tag and pulled them over my pink, wrinkled, *Imperial Leather* soaked feet. The brogues were comfortable leather and hardly worn.

Could this really be me? I thought, catching sight of my reflection in a piece of broken mirror resting against the barn timbers – clean shaven, shining hair, dressed if not to kill at least to threaten.

At this stage I hadn't really wondered how I would be expected to pay for any of this: I had already forgotten I was only here to apply for a job, mucking out horses.

The barn door opened again and I caught sight of my old clothes going up in smoke in a tin dustbin in the yard.

"So there is a person under all that filth?" she said. I was about to object but didn't get the chance.
"Dinner in half an hour, then I'll show you the ropes."

The ropes turned out to be the cook and the butler who both, after supplying and serving us with a delicious five-course dinner, were given the night off.

Assuming that I would be sleeping in the barn, as had always been the case in the past when I had taken on casual labouring for a few days, I stood up from the table to leave.

Mrs Redrum wiped the corners of her mouth delicately with a white linen napkin. Dressed for dinner, she did not look half as formidable as she had in her jodhpurs.

"I'll show you to your room," she said, leading the way.

I tried not to look too over-awed at the sight of the four-poster. I tried to look as if I spent every night between clean, crisp sheets.

"I'll be up to make an early start for you," I told her. "I'm an early riser any time."

"Really?" she said. "That's interesting."

She departed, leaving a mixed scent in the air – of horses and grilled steak and fried onions.

I snuggled down under the covers, listening to the cistern in the bathroom next door filling up as she took a shower. A warm floaty cloud drifted over me. My eyelids became heavy, and I sank into a delicious sleep.

I was awakened by a tigress in bed beside me.

"Thought you might like someone to keep you warm," Mrs Redrum whispered as she snuggled up to me. The cuddle was short-lived. Soon she was a raging animal, firm breasts smothering me, fingernails scratching me. She was insatiable.

Usually it's the woman that caves in on such occasions, but in the end I had to tell her that if I was going to do any mucking out in her stables next day she would have to let me get some rest. She departed, chuckling.

It was still dark when the housekeeper woke me the following morning.

"It's six," she said, disgusted that I was still in bed at that hour. "Breakfast's been on the table for half an hour."

She was good to me, Mrs. Redrum. She visited me nightly, and by way of a bonus, in the feed store, the back of the Landrover, the barn. Whenever I saw the stallions performing I ran for cover. But she would always seek me out.

"How long has your husband been dead?" I asked when I thought I knew her well enough to enquire.
"Whatever gave you that idea?" she said. "He's not dead. We were not compatible. He got a lot of headaches. In the end he ran off with his headache and one of the stable boys."

I began to get nervous when she talked about things we could do "in the spring" or "next summer" – I didn't like plans. They frightened me. That's why I'd taken to the road in the first place, so as not to be tied to plans. I'd enjoyed the little interlude with Mrs Redrum greatly and I felt a bit guilty about this urge to move on. But soon after that – she'd been in my bed for a couple of hours one night and had gone to sleep – I slipped into my corduroy trousers and thick woollen jacket and departed before dawn. I left a note for her to find. The least I could do was to thank her.

For a time I was the best-dressed tramp in the land.

CHAPTER 15
Halfway House

My companion on the dry-stone wall stood up and stretched his legs. "I'd best be on my way," he said. "I can't tell you how much I've enjoyed listening to your tales. And you've given me a bit of hope for the future. So let the Gas Board take the car back – I don't care." He held out his hand to shake mine. He clasped both hands around my hand shaking it vigorously.

"Good luck," he said, thrusting a hand into his pocket and taking out a fiver. "Have a drink on me, friend."

As he made towards his car I felt a strange melancholy sweeping through me. To my own surprise, I'd enjoyed his company these past couple of days and I suddenly felt alone, even though I know I am not alone – there are lots like me.

At that moment – when he reached his car and turned and waved, I wanted to be with people.

* * * *

I joined the trickle of weary travellers drifting towards the gates of Halfway House. Tired and footsore from the long walk into town, I made my way with them not only to the warmth and shelter that Halfway House offered but to the comfort of the companionship of other wayfarers.

I had passed through its door only once before, when I had felt alone and depressed, and I had left uplifted.

There was no disguising the fact that Halfway House was all that was left of the old workhouse. On the green and cream walls of the long corridor were messages left by passers-through. I wondered as I made my way to the kitchen what level of IQ my fellow-vagrants possessed. The author of "I wear my sister's knickers" obviously didn't have any underwear of his own. And I later found out that the scribbler of the message "Meet me in the bogs after lights out" had been found beaten up and dumped in a cubicle. One slogan that had been there on the urinal wall on my last visit round about Christmas was still there "Season's greetings to all our readers."

The place was little more than a dump. No amount of disinfectant could eradicate the stench of dank mattresses and dirty bodies, and the red polish – so favoured by institutions – did nothing to improve the cracked and worn lino.

But after weeks of sleeping in shop doorways, bus shelters, park benches and derelict property, Halfway House was the nearest thing to home that many of its floating population would ever know.

Some, unused to company and unable to communicate or to be communicated with, simply sat staring at the walls enjoying the warmth. Others played cards and joined in raucous merriment with friends not seen for many a week.

There were few rules, but those that there were had to be obeyed. One was a shower before bedding down. This of course was more in an attempt to keep the beds clean than to rid the travellers of unwanted inhabitants of their skin and hair. Another was no alcohol. And another lights out at ten thirty. But the most hard-to-accept rule was that you were only allowed to stay one night. It was looked upon by most as a one-night luxury that set them up for the days ahead.

Though it was not a rule at Halfway House, most of the travellers made an attempt to leave the little area that had been theirs for the night in a state fit for the next weary body. But many of the visitors were chronic alcoholics with little control over their bladders, so that it was a losing battle the charity had to face in trying to rid the place of the stench of urine.

Four hours after lights out I was still awake. It wasn't so much the noise – the snoring, the coughing, the spitting, the farting – that kept me from sleep. It was that ever-pervading smell of urine in my nostrils. Norman had said the same about being in prison, I remembered.

"Can't sleep, eh?" the man in the next bed asked in an accent I found difficult to pinpoint. "Me neither. It's like being in a zoo."

I could hear an old man at the top of the room, talking to himself, re-living the Normandy landings and shouting to his long-dead friends to watch out.

"Jock," the bloke in the next bed held out his hand. No-one ever asked for second names.
"Poor old sod," I said nodding my head in the direction of the war hero screaming at his army friends to get the hell out of there. "Did his bit now no bugger wants him."

Jock nodded his head in agreement.

"Still, I hope I never get that bad," he said.
"Who knows how any of us will end up?" I asked, not expecting a reply.

Jock's wife, it seemed, had died twenty years ago. I put him at around fifty, though it's difficult to gauge the age of travellers, their faces chiselled by the winds and cooked by the sun. He had taken to the road and been unable to settle since.

Before the war he had been a jeweller. He had his own business. He could mend watches, repair gold chains, expand ruby rings to fit the ever-fattening fingers of the aristocracy.

"Then when Hitler rounded up the Jews in Berlin, I was sent with all the others to a concentration camp."

"You're a German Jew?" I asked astonished. He nodded, put his index finger to his lips and whispered,

"Shush." Then he laughed. "A Jew with a name like Jock, good cover, eh?"

He lit up a cigarette and offered me one. I shook my head.

"Like a million others," he continued, "I expected to be sent to the gas chamber. We'd huddle together, all skin and bone, awaiting our fates at the hands of our captors, like scared rabbits cornered in a hole with no way out."

Usually I was the story-teller – this was an unexpected turn – and I was hooked on his memories, sad though they were.

"One night a guard thundered into our hut, and pointed that terrifying finger – at me. 'You!' he bellowed, 'come with me.'

I got to my feet and followed, stretching out a skeletal hand to say goodbye to the few friends I had left.

The guard strode out in the direction of the commandant's quarters. I struggled to keep up with him – he was tall and strong and well fed – I was anything but.

The commandant was sitting at a table strewn with papers and pewter tankards and odds and ends of jewellery. He looked up as I entered behind the guard. He motioned to my escort to leave us alone. The guard obeyed.

For what seemed a long time but was probably only moments, he stared at me in silence, and then cleared his throat.

"You were a jeweller, yes?" he asked.

"Yes sir," I said.

"I have work for you," he said, pushing across the table a cigar box. My stomach fell into my naked feet, for the box contained the gold teeth and fillings prised from the jaws of my fellow prisoners before their bodies were bulldozed into a mass grave.

"Well?" he asked. "What do you see?"

"I see, er, gold, sir."

"Good," he said. "And what can you do with such gold?"

"Whatever you want me to do with it, sir."

"Well I'll tell you what I want," he went on. "I want you, a jeweller, to take this gold and make it into rings."

There was no doubt in my mind that the gold would, in some form or another, be spirited away to await the end of the war.

"Do you think you can do that?" he said, standing up and lashing the table with his stick. He leant towards me so that his face was almost touching mine.

"Well?" he asked menacingly.

He said it as if offering me a choice, but the choice was not mine to make, not if I was to escape the fate of so many other prisoners.

"I will do my very best," I told him.

He despatched me to the hospital and I tasted for the first time in many long months the warmth of broth and the sweetness of eggs. This new diet proved too rich for a stomach so long deprived, but day by day I began to hold the food down, and enjoy it.

I set about the task I had been given, knowing that it could be my salvation. I made rings and chain bracelets and simple, small ingots on which I engraved dates and initials to his command. I decided one day to fashion him a pen. It would take a lot of gold, I knew that, and a lot of work, but I was prepared to do it, not simply to keep on the better side of the commandant but because the work filled me with pride and occupied my hands and mind. I kept the pen hidden until it was completed, and then presented it to him. He was delighted.

The guards lost no time in acquainting my fellow inmates of my action and I became very unpopular. I knew that later on they would thank me, but for the time being I had to put up with their jibes and then worse, with their ignoring me.

Rumour had it that the Allies were closing in. The camp commandant, who, I had noticed sucked the end of his pens when he was faced with a problem, sat behind the table in his quarters studying the notes before him.

It took only seconds. A strong, powerful man he might have been, but within seconds he was writhing in agony on the floor screaming for the guards. Unlike my friends, who had filed to the gas chambers in silence, he departed the land of the living crying and screaming.

The idea had come to me when I'd been sent to the stores one day to collect the commandant's bread. I had noticed a large tin on a shelf, skull and crossbones stencilled on its side. Also on the shelf was a large rat, recently expired, having devoured the crystals that had been spilled onto the shelf from the tin. While the guard was fetching the bread from the back of the hut, I quickly scooped what was left of the crystals into my hand, and once outside the store I emptied them into the little secret pocket I had made inside the top of my trousers. Back in the hut I found a dry place under my bunk against the wall.

At the time I had simply thought that if I outlived my usefulness for the commandant, it would be a better way out than the gas chamber.

But that was before I made the pen.

I crushed the crystals and with my fingers painted them onto the end of the gold pen. Yes, it took only seconds.

By the time the guard arrived, the commandant's body was still and he was quite, quite dead.

"Cowardly bastard," the guard declared. "Decided to get out while the going was good." At the sound of hurrying footsteps outside, the guard bent down and pocketed the gold pen. His body was not found till the following day, when the guard who found him bent down and pocketed the pen.

I chuckled to myself thinking that this pen could be responsible for wiping out the whole German army.

The Allies arrived. We were saved, those of us who were left.

A few of us made for England.

It took a while to adjust, but finally I settled and married a wonderful Jewish woman. Together we worked hard, and our hard work paid off for our business prospered. I was happier than I had ever been. And I believed she was too.

I closed up the shop early one evening, and hurried home hoping to arrive before she had made a start on preparing dinner. "I am taking you out, my love," I was rehearsing in my mind as I walked quickly along the pavement. "We have reached our little goal at the shop, and we are dining out!" I knew she would be pleased on both counts.

I shook the rain from my coat as I entered the hall of the house. I called. But there was no answer. And then I heard ... the noises coming from upstairs ... not noises of pain or anguish, but of sheer delight and ecstasy.

In that moment my world collapsed.

I was no match for the bronzed, virile youth who was jumping around in my bed.

I had lived through the camps, through the war, through the prejudice, but now I had to muster all my inner strength to live through this.

I crept back down the stairs and out into the rain. I walked around until it was the usual hour for me to return home. I pushed the incident further and further down into my stomach and refused to let it escape. It was never mentioned.

Then some weeks later, I returned from the shop and entered the hall to the smell of a veritable kosher banquet. Our tastes had always been simple, our appetites having weakened during the war years.

"What's this?" I asked. "Are we celebrating?"

She was standing at the top of the stairs looking radiant. We met. She on the way down and I on the way up. She flung her arms around me.
"I'm pregnant," she announced, with unimaginable excitement in her voice and happiness in her eyes.

It took only the merest of pushes – no more than a prod really. I stood and watched, almost outside myself, as her body bounced like a rubber ball down the uncarpeted staircase. She didn't make a sound – not even when I bent over her.

"You betrayed me," I told her simply. The look of pure hatred was in her eyes as the last gasps hissed from her mouth.

It was that easy.

Once I was sure she was dead, I rang for an ambulance. The police arrived just before it. My performance in the next couple of hours would have put me high on the Oscars list, I can tell you. Tears streamed down my face, I turned down all offers of comfort, I even threatened suicide.

The verdict was "accidental death" ... so sad, especially since the autopsy had revealed she was pregnant with our first child, and after trying for so many years too. Funny that, considering the commandant back there had seen to it that I would never father children – they'd call it having the snip these days, then they called it something else.

I sold up after that. I saw a solicitor and made a will – everything to the RSPCA – after all, animals don't let you down, animals are faithful no matter what.

"Stop nattering, you two!" an inmate of Halfway House shouted in our direction. "Some of us want to get some sleep."

When I woke in the morning Jock had gone.

It was a month later that I learned by bush telegraph that he had been found dead on the back seat of a bus in Newcastle.

CHAPTER 16

Real Men Don't Cry

There are some stories that are not for the telling, not for the sharing, but for keeping only to oneself, in the deep dark corners of the mind – to dance through and savour again on rainy days ... and to wonder what might have been.

* * * *

I have to admit there are times when I get a bit down, feel a bit sorry for myself. But then don't we all?

The rain was running down my neck, the nail in my boot had driven its way into the heel of my foot, and I felt pretty miserable. I knew a pint would put my mood to rights, but the pub looked posh – you know, the sort of country pub that once welcomed farmers in their dirt with their dogs but now welcome only the landed gentry and townies out for a meal. One look at me, I thought, and they'll throw me out.

"Coming in?" a voice behind me asked. "I'll buy you a pint." This perfect stranger ushered me through the door of the pub. "Pint of bitter for me and whatever this here chap wants, Jack," he said. The landlord never batted an eyelid.

"What'll it be then, sir?" he asked me.

Beside the pint on the bar that he drew for me the landlord placed a paper serviette with a ham sandwich inside. "On the house," he said with a nod of the head.

They must have seen how down I was, how desperate I felt just at that time. In a town, people would have ignored me or pitched me out. True country people notice.

At the end of the lane was a disused shed. I entered it cautiously, wondering if this would be another hen house like the one I'd sheltered in before. I took off my rucksack and unrolled my sleeping bag. I put back inside the rucksack the sandwich in foil that the landlord had given me "for breakfast" he'd said.

I lay there unable to sleep, and my thoughts inevitably turned to Jean. She had been my first (and only, if truth be known) true love. Thank God she can't see me now, I thought.

I'd met Jean whilst on a holiday in Cornwall. Edna had gone to her mother's in York for a couple of weeks so I went down to our beach house in St Ives.

Jean lived in Cornwall and worked in the office of a local building firm. She had been sitting on a bench at the top of the cliffs eating an apple, and I was returning to our beach house after a long morning walk.

I was instantly smitten.

She had long, dark hair which she fingered nervously and which shyness I found attractive. She was neither slim nor plump but curvaceous and quietly vivacious. There was an air about her that knocked me out. I can smell her perfume even now.

"Mind if I join you?" I asked, presumptuously sitting down on the bench beside her. She edged away a little along the seat, and I hastened to assure her I meant no harm.
"I'm on holiday for a couple of weeks. You?"
"No," she said timidly. "I live here. It's my lunchtime from work. And I really must be getting back now."

And she was gone.

I could hardly wait for next day, hoping the spot on the cliff top was her regular lunch-time haunt. I hung around a little way from the bench, hiding (I must shamefully admit) in a shallow hollow. When she arrived I approached casually as if this second meeting was simply a coincidence.

"We meet again," I smiled, sitting down beside her on the bench. She seemed more relaxed today, not so intimidated as before.
"Come here often?" I teased.
She smiled. "Every weekday for lunch," she said.

Each lunch time that week we met and chatted, and eventually I plucked up courage to ask her out on a date. She looked taken aback.

"I thought you said you were married?" she sounded reproachful. "And I told you, I have a boy friend."

"Is that a yes or a no then?" I asked tentatively
"No," she said quite definitely. My heart sank.

On the Saturday and Sunday of that first week I still went by the bench at the top of the cliff but there was no sign of Jean.

By the Monday I was beginning to fear I would never see her again. But she arrived with her lunch just as I reached the bench on the cliff.

My insistence, thankfully, wore her down, and she agreed to let me take her to dinner one night during that second week of my holiday.

I'll never forget that evening: the air was still warm from the day's sun, and the moors were alive with greens and yellows and browns. I picked her up at the harbour and, at my insistence that she should choose, she directed me to a quiet little eating inn on the road out of St Ives.

The Smugglers' Rest had, for many years, been disused and had become derelict, But then some enterprising chap from Manchester had taken it on and managed to refurbish it in a style that seemed old and authentic and totally in keeping with its surroundings. A mixture of candlelight and subdued concealed lighting created an atmosphere of intimacy.

We didn't rush the meal. The light from the candle played on Jean's gentle features, just a little flushed from the wine. I can see her now. Radiant and smiling.

The old grandfather clock in the corner struck ten and interrupted our reveries. Neither of us wanted to make a move, but we knew we must.

It was a magical drive over the moors that night. The moon bathed the landscape in silver and the road was a thin ribbon stretching into the distance.

"It's just a little bit further," Jean said, directing me to her house. I pulled into the side of the road. It was dark and quiet ... there was not a sound either outside the car or inside it. Then without warning Jean snuggled up to me. With my hand on her cheek I lifted her face towards me and kissed her, gently and tenderly. The response was all I had wished for. I smothered my face in the richness of her thick, scented hair as my hands sought to caress her breasts beneath the white satin blouse.

Jean pulled away quickly.

"This is not right," she said, almost in tears. "We shouldn't be here, doing this, it's wrong."

In a second she was out of the car and running down the moon-lit avenue.

But the following lunchtime, to my relief, she appeared at the bench on the top of the cliffs.

"I'm sorry about last night," she said. "There's no future for us. You see, we've set the date – 14th of next month. Everything's arranged."

I took hold of her hand. I smiled though inside I was screaming. I stood up and took her into my arms.

"No, no," she was sobbing now. "I have to go."
"Please," I could hear myself pleading. But she pulled away and ran off.

On the Thursday of that second week of my holiday, I arrived at the bench and found a note.

I won't be here today – have to work through the lunch time. But I'm having tomorrow off. We can have the whole day together and then she had added as if an afterthought *if you like. I'll be here at ten.*

Ten the following morning could not come soon enough for me, but then it went all too quickly.

We walked along the cliffs. Even the sun was hiding behind a thin covering of cloud as if it knew this was not a day for sunshine.

Almost reclaimed by moor grass, the little-used path took a right turn. Protected by rocks and completely hidden from view the tiny grass-filled hollow was still warm. I pulled Jean down beside me on the warm-smelling, dark earth. Her skin was soft and smooth beneath my fingers, her lips warm and gentle, and her hair smelled of indescribable flowers. Desperately, we clung together, me kissing away her tears.

My trembling fingers unbuttoned her blouse. She offered no resistance, but took my hand and slid it beneath to feel the smooth rise of her breasts there. I gazed in wonderment at her beautiful naked body. And we were together at last.

Her words as we lay entwined together will be with me for ever.

"Love me, love me," she begged, "make this my day to remember". As that moment came upon us that would overshadow all others, we knew that nothing had been or could ever be as beautiful as this declaration of love.

We lay there curled around each other, Jean's hair spread in a fine web on my face and her fingers drawing patterns on my bare shoulders. I wanted so much to take her to the beach house, to build a fire in the old grate and make love to her in its flickering warmth.

I gazed now at this precious life in my arms.

Her smooth, damp body trembled and I drew her near in a fond caress. It was then that I discovered tears really do taste of salt.

No words were needed. We both of us knew that life would never be the same again, that somewhere in the deep dark places we keep hidden in our minds, we would creep across each other's dreams, wondering what might have been.

So real men don't cry, eh? Well, I cried. I cried then, and sometimes even now. I had known her for less than two weeks, but the scent of her body, the coolness of her skin, her shy little smile as she twirled her hair around her fingers – they would remain with me for ever.

CHAPTER 17

The Inconsiderate Sod

I made my way down into the village before it got dark. In a corner of the Dun Cow I was sitting enjoying a pint paid for by the landlord (on condition that I hopped it when the regulars started to arrive) when I caught sight of myself in one of those pictures that are painted onto mirrors. The painted picture didn't cover the whole mirror and I saw the reflection of this un-shaven, shaggy-haired tramp that was me. With one hand on my pint, the other stroked the bristles on my face. I finished my pint quickly. I didn't want anyone who might know me from my accounting days to walk into the pub and see me. Was it all that long since I had been happy to spend time in this pub in the company of friends?

* * * *

Derek Dudley blew into the pub in a paddy.

"Can't move for bloody ambulances out there," he loudly complained. "Some inconsiderate sod has parked his car on the railway tracks."

The landlord looked aghast.

"Was he in it?" he asked.
"Who?" Derek Dudley said in all innocence.
"The inconsiderate sod!" he said.
"God knows, Jack. Give us a pint."

For once it seemed Derek Dudley was buying his own pint. He had this annoying habit of waiting till your back was turned and then emptying any glass on the table proclaiming he thought it was his. More often than not he escaped a kick in the goolies only because he was six-foot-four in his stocking feet.

"I'll teach him one o' these days," said Arnold Ramsbottom, frequenter of public houses and dog tracks.

Arnold kept greyhounds; they certainly didn't keep him, except in a state of poverty.

He'd received the usual ultimatum from his wife some weeks previously.

"Get those dogs out of my bedroom or I leave," she had warned him.
"So how are you managing on your own these days?" the landlord asked sarcastically.

Arnold didn't reply. His eyes had glazed over. The barmaid had leant down to collect glasses from the table and his blinkered vision had homed in on the bit of flesh that was showing at the front of her blouse. His teeth began chattering like the jaws of his greyhound, Dancer, whenever there was a bitch on heat within a hundred yards of it. The barmaid stood up, but it was some time before Arnold regained control of his eyeballs.

Derek Dudley was leaning on the bar, finishing off his pint.

Arnold, whose automatic reflex action was about to go into motion to finish his half-full glass before Derek Dudley reached the table, called to him to join us.

It was obvious to me, though not to Derek Dudley, just what Arnold was up to. Within minutes of Derek sitting down, Arnold lifted the leg of the table and trapped Dancer's lead in it, and then stood up claiming a call of nature needed to be answered and made for the Gents.

The metaphorical trap-door had opened, and Derek fell straight in. He leant across to take Arnold's unfinished glass, raised it to his lips and drank.

'Course what he did not know is that as soon as Arnold had spied him arriving, he had sprinkled a crushed tablet into the half-full glass – one of Dancer's worming tablets.

Dudley left early.

Arnold was shaking with laughter as we made our way out of the pub. The flashing lights of ambulances and police cars had a strobe effect on me and Arnold but worse than that they startled his dog and it set off, taking him with it.

I leant over the parapet to see what was going on down on the railway line. The medics were zipping up a body bag presumably containing the remains of the poor sod from the car and the police were imposing their presence on anyone who tried to venture within fifty yards. Three of them were squabbling about determining the boundaries of the accident scene with yellow tape.

From nowhere Bijou, Derek Dudley's poodle bitch appeared, being hotly pursued by the unbridled Dancer. There was no sign of either Derek or Arnold though I could hear a voice screaming at the empassioned Dancer to leave his bitch alone. Bijou ran straight through what seemed to be the entire police force of the town, totally ignoring their yellow tape and signs to keep out. But the greyhound stopped, surveyed for a moment the largest of the constabulary and then uncharacteristically sank its teeth into the hand that was waving the yellow tape.

Arnold appeared now and running straight through the tape screamed *en route*, "Has anybody seen my Dancer?"

The wounded policeman was making his way towards an ambulance, nursing his arm and wailing to the medic escorting him, "No, I can't remember when I last had a bloody tetanus jab."

The body bag had nearly reached an ambulance.

"Do we know who it is?" I asked one of the bearers.

"Chap called Entwistle, I believe," he said. Yet another copper was telling me to buzz off.

"Not Ernie Entwistle?" I said.

"I said get behind the tape!" PC-in-charge-of-body-bag ordered me.

On my way to the Dun Cow only that night, I'd caught up with Ernie. I could see he was upset about something and he was only too eager to tell me.

"Maggie's got a toy boy."

"You sure?" I asked. His look was contemptuous.

"Window cleaner – nobbut a kid."

Ernie was around ten stone wet through: Maggie was around seventeen stone bone dry. She had no personality, no figure, no looks, very little hair, no patience and no front teeth. I had never understood what Ernie saw in her, but surely any self-respecting window cleaner could do better.

"I went bird-watching last Sunday. I got back early – I was watching a sparrow hawk circle when it evacuated its bowels." (A less cultured twitcher might have said the bugger had shit in his eye, but not Ernie.)

"I could hear 'em at it when I got in, and what do you think she said?" He looked at me, waiting for some sort of response, but how was I to know what the hell she had said?

"Well I'll tell you," he told me, "she said 'I'll get you the Optrex dear' – that's what she said."

"Well, I'll be buggered ..." I began, then stopped in mid-flow when I noticed he was on the verge of tears – and that I definitely could not cope with.

"Hope you told her to bugger off then," I consoled him. There was a loud sniff and I hastened to bring the conversation to an end.

"I'll hurry on to the Dun Cow and get 'em in, Ernie. You take your time, friend."

Some friend, eh? He must have gone back to his car and decided enough was enough.

Derek Dudley pushed past me carrying his little white poodle whose hind quarters appeared to be caked in mud. He walked headlong into the yellow plastic tape which nearly throttled the dog. He snatched at the tape furiously, tore at it and grunted in the direction of the smashed car still strewn across the railway line,

"Inconsiderate sod!"

CHAPTER 18

The Little People

Irish whiskey is not like any other – I mean the spirit, not of the ghost or un-dead variety, but of the illegally distilled liquor type. Two glasses of the stuff and you could believe you could walk on water. In fact, you could believe almost anything.

* * * *

Sometimes, particularly in the winter, I would venture into town just to soak up the warmth in the shopping precinct. I would find an empty bench and sit down; each bench seat was meant to accommodate half a dozen people, but my very presence on one deterred shoppers from resting their weary loads anywhere near mine. Far from being offended, I was glad to be left alone. They had warm homes to go to, warm cars to drive home in. How could they appreciate the gentle permeating warmth as I did?

It was on one such day in mid-November that I sat on a bench in the Spindles Shopping Precinct, watching the world and his dog go by.

"By hell, is that you?" a voice said, bending to get a better look at my face. "By hell it is, isn't it? It's you."
"It's me, all right, Harold," I said.
"On yer feet, lad," he said. "Let's go and get sommat to eat."
"Tell you what," I said, remaining seated on the bench, "you go and get sommat and I'll wait here – they're not so keen on us gentlemen of the road muckying up their chintz in the cafe."

Harold Wolstenholme returned within minutes, with sandwiches in a couple of paper bags that were printed with pictures of olde world shoppes. I hoped their sandwiches were more up to date.

"I'd heard you'd gone off to see the world once the redundancy money had run out," he laughed. "How much of it have you seen?"

Harold had once been a neighbour, in my married, working days. We had never actually been friends, but funnily enough we talked as friends now. Despite the body-odour I must have been giving off, he did not move obviously up-wind of me and didn't seem to notice shoppers tut-tutting at me as they passed by.

"So," he said after about half an hour of skirting around trivial issues, "where do you lay your weary head o' nights?"

"Well," I said truthfully, "there's a nice little derelict barn up by High Moor that I've used a time or two in the past – it's dry and warm..."

"Tell you what," he interrupted. "I'm off to Ireland tomorrow to look at some dogs. Still interested in dogs?"

He knew the answer. I shrugged and nodded

"There's room in the van if you fancy a free trip across to the Emerald Isle. You can sleep at ours tonight, and we'll make an early start in the morning. Come on then. Let's be having you."

And with that, he put a strong arm under my elbow and nearly lifted me off my feet.

"Course you'll have to have a bath. You don't mind me saying, do you?"

I smiled.

"No, I don't mind you saying at all. But what about your wife? What will she have to say?"

"Not set eyes on her for a helluva while. She cleared off with a feller that preferred cats to dogs. I ask yer – what sort of feller prefers cats to dogs? Anyway she persuaded him to buy a bull terrier and apparently it bit her in the arse one night. Seems she turned instantly and bit the bugger back. They had to have it put down."

I was not following the logic of all this very well, but knowing his wife I could well imagine her not thinking twice about biting a bull terrier – she had been known to chew the odd bit of flesh off Harold.

The prospect of a warm bath and a warm bed for the night sounded more than all right to me and I was grateful. The coming trip to Ireland and in the company of greyhounds, seemed almost too wonderful for words.

We passed the house I had occupied with Edna. The paint on the door and window frames had flaked off in places so that they had a piebald look about them. Though the windows were boarded up, the vandals had had a field day. The chipboard where once there was glass was covered in *graffiti*. The door had a spray-painted message presumably directed at anyone and everyone – advising that they should go away and procreate.

I knew that Harold had put a spring in his step to hurry past, hoping to save me from something – sadness, embarrassment, disgust, whatever. But he needn't have bothered. I had no regrets.

In the intervening years, his sons had grown up and left home. He maintained contact with them and photographs of them and their wives and the odd youngster were all about the place. It was untidy, as places get when there is no woman around, but who was I to complain?

We talked long into the night. We started with curry and chips, then coffee, then toast, then coffee, then…. sleep ... long, warm, delicious sleep.

"These'll be too long for a midget like you," Harold told me in the morning, throwing a pair of thick jeans onto the bed, "but you can roll 'em up at the bottom. And there's some woollies there – tekk yer pick."

Though obviously not new, the clothes had a lot of wear still left in them. I dressed quickly and followed the smell of bacon and eggs that had sifted up the stairs. Harold was at the cooker with half a dozen eggs frying in the pan.

"Ah now tha looks like an accountant agin," he said. "I don't want you looking like a tramp."

"I am a tramp, Harold," I said.

"Not while yer with me, yer not," he insisted. And looking at him, he looked more like a tramp than I did.

"Could be last decent meal we get before we reach Ireland," he said, splitting the eggs with a fish splice and lifting three of them onto a plate already full of rashers and sausages.

"Get that down yer, then we'd best tekk the dogs for a walk afore we set off." He noticed my slightly quizzical look. "Can't leave 'em behind here – who'd tekk care of 'em? That owd cow next door'd let 'em starve afore she'd see to 'em. Tessa here chased a cat through her kitchen one day and knocked sommat off her old mantelpiece in there – seems it was her old man's ashes. She's not spoken civilly to me or the dogs since." He was gathering dog leads for the two dogs from a hook behind the door. He handed me one.

"You tekk Tessa. She's gentle." He collared the bigger of the two animals and clipped on the lead "Be gentle with him, Tessa mi love," he laughed in the dog's ear. "I'll tekk Bruno, he's a bit of a handful."

Later in the van *en route* to the ferry at Holyhead I came to understand just how much of a handful Bruno was. He would insist that my leg was a bitch on heat and in the end I had to persuade him, ever so gently with a word in his ear and a kick in the goolies, that it was not.

The crossing was smooth, the sea was calm, like a park lake as they say.

I was not ... my stomach was not ... my bowels were not...

"I believe you," I told Harold when he insisted on telling me what breath-taking landscapes we were passing through on arrival in Ireland. When I finally gained control of my own body, I agreed with everything he was saying. But while Harold was silently praying to get his hands on a couple of good dogs, I was praying to the same God for a safe and calm passage home.

News of our visit and the purpose thereof travelled fast. Owners from all over the county arrived at the bar declaring their dogs to be the best in Ireland. I wondered where all the slow dogs were, for if any of these silver-tongued breeders were to be believed then every dog in Ireland was bred-in-the-purple and a potential Classics winner.

It took us a week to do the rounds of the various dog breeders' kennels. Each night back at the Greyhound Inn, Harold studied his copious notes on each of the dogs he had inspected. After changing his mind several times, he eventually narrowed the list down to four and finally settled on two.

"Lady of the Isles is her racing name," the bitch's proud owner told us, "but we call her 'Peg-legs,' the youngest of his offspring shouted from the house.

"It's just his little joke," his father smiled, but I noticed the dog pricked up its ears. "Peggoty, is her pet name. She'll not let you down." He pocketed the hundred English notes without counting them. "You won't regret it," he said, then turned towards the house to see his youngest child bolting for the fields before his father could catch him.

"I'll tekk her," Harold said, and the man pocketed the money gratefully.

Bernard of Blarney was a sleek, elegant dog that looked as if he could win races even if his owner was lying that he had.

Mr Blarney-stone was getting a little anxious watching Harold examining the hound at close quarters.

"Can my good wife offer you a hearty breakfast, gents?" he asked, hoping to divert too close an inspection of the dog.

Harold stood back, looking hard at the dog and stroking his chin where a two-day growth of stubble was bordering on becoming a beard.

"I'll tekk him," Harold said at last, and though Harold did not notice, I did – the look of relief and satisfaction on Mr Blarney-stone's face. So the bargain was struck.

The animal seemed reluctant to leave his owner, but eventually we got him into the van.

Harold's two dogs from home were allowed in the Inn and slept on the floor in our room

The plan was that we would be returning to England the next day, so we – Harold – decided we would have a good night out to celebrate his purchases and the fortune he just knew would be coming his way when these two bred-in-the-purple greyhounds earned their wages back home.

The last I saw of Harold that night he was stripped down to his underpants rendering (in all honesty I could not say singing) *Danny Boy* and swaying precariously on the bar top at the Greyhound Inn.

"He's well away," the landlord said at closing time. "I'll lock up and leave him on the floor" (where Harold had quietly sunk at the end of his rendition) "and we'll go on to O'Leary's place for a night-cap."

I didn't know and didn't care who O'Leary was. I'd already had more than a sniff of the powerful whiskey and was walking on clouds and imagined I could even walk on water.

"Come on then," the landlord said, shutting off the lights at the Greyhound Inn and closing the door with us on the pavement outside. I obeyed. But scarcely had I got my breath back from a slip against an empty beer barrel on the pavement, than the landlord had disappeared out of sight. Still, that presented no problem to one who could walk on water. He had said "up here" pointing up there, so I set off up the street.

Whether someone or something hit me – the air, the whiskey, a jealous dog breeder – I will never know. But the next time I opened my eyes I was lying in a puddle and someone was tugging at my trouser leg.

"Now you can't be spending the night in a puddle," a voice was whispering to me. I looked up from the gutter to see a small person clad in green with a pointed hat that flopped to one side with a bell on the end. Now I knew I was drunk. But the tugging at my trouser leg was insistent.
"Tis my job to take care of ye, and take care of ye I will," he persisted.

If he'd been any bigger than two feet two I'd have told him where to go in no uncertain terms, as it was I succumbed to the sweet breath of whiskey and drifted into sleep.

In that gutter that night I dreamt of partying with leprechauns – drinking sweet nectar from dock leaves and eating red, juicy berries. I sang and danced in a circle of little people, all happy and laughing and making merry. A round, jolly woman handed me some sort of carving and I put it in my pocket. I dreamed a dream of laughter and love.

I woke up on the pavement outside the Greyhound Inn covered in a layer of dry autumn leaves in the middle of November. How I came to be there I never did find out.

Inside the Inn Harold had woken up, showered and shaved and was ready for the homeward journey.

That morning was chaotic. Harold's two dogs from home, and the recently-acquired Lady of the Isles and Bernard of Blarney took an instant dislike to each other. Skin and hair were flying as we tried in vain to persuade them to accept each other as travelling companions.

Bernard of Blarney had a mind of his own. In transit to the van – that is, me dragging him for all I was worth and him resisting like a ten-ton truck – he decided to part company with me and the collar I was holding onto and set off at the speed of light down the village road. By hell, could that dog run. His owner was right, he certainly had it in him to win the classic, if he could just be persuaded not to keep running home.

The landlord was standing in the Inn doorway watching the proceedings.

"One born every minute," he laughed. "You'll not be seeing that dog again lads. It's trained to go home the first chance it gets and believe me it never gets further than here. He must have sold it a dozen times."

Harold was furious, but there was no time to search for the dog – the ferry would be leaving without us if we didn't make our way there quickly.

"You can tell that bloody dog-breeder that I'll be back to collect my purchase," he said. He slammed the van door to and crashed into gear.

"And where the hell did you get to last night?" he asked me.

"If I told you I didn't know, would you believe me?" I said. He laughed out loud.

"I'll tell you what," he said, "that bloody home-grown whiskey is powerful stuff all right."

He was still laughing when I put my hand in my pocket and felt there a small carving of a little leprechaun.

CHAPTER 19

Dead Men's Shoes

I parted company with Harold Wolstenholme and his three greyhounds almost as soon as we arrived back in Yorkshire. I wished him well with his new, bred-in-the-purple Lady of the Isles and he wished me well on my travels.

* * * *

It was getting near to Christmas. There was a bite in the easterly wind that blew through the gap in the Pennines with nothing to stop it between Huddersfield and Manchester. The first snow had hardly covered the ground and it had taken but a weak, watery, winter sun to dissolve it into the earth and the drains. But the skies were heavy with more to come, and the wind whistled through the timbers of the derelict barn I had come to regard as home.

A trip into town to warm up in the shopping mall seemed like a good idea.

The shops were festooned with lights and garlands and tinsel, and piped music told me that Santa Claus was coming to town. As soon as I'd thawed out, I zipped up the woollen jacket Harold had insisted on giving me and tied a thick, woollen scarf around my middle, ready to hurry back to my hillside hide-away.

It was getting dark when I neared the Mill on the edge of town. I sat down for a minute before beginning the long climb back up the hills to "home."

"I don't pay you to hang about! Pull your finger out and get this yard cleared up before it gets pitch black!"

He was right of course – he didn't pay me, because I didn't work for him.

A chap in blue overalls came scurrying round the corner.

"Daft as a brush," he said nodding in the direction of my accuser as he disappeared through the door into the reception office of the Mill. "Silly sod thinks you work for him."
"Well, I don't," I assured him.
The man chuckled. "And neither will I for much longer. I retire next week."

Now whilst the job of cleaning up a yard every night didn't particularly appeal to me, funds were at an all-time low and a bit of spare cash in my pocket would be handy. The man in the yard could read my thoughts.

"If you want the job, now's the time to grab it before someone else does."

And so for a short while I became a part-time yard sweeper-upper or to quote the manager "that idle bugger in the yard."

No, you could safely say that Mr James Lomas, Owner/Manager of Mason's Carpets, certainly did not take to me – nor I to him. But he could not deny that the yard was kept cleaner and tidier than it had ever been.

He was a giant of a man – six feet two, seventeen stones, with huge hands and big feet, and a temper to match. But it hadn't always been so. In his young days he had been a creep, and indeed that is how he came to be Manager, for he spent his days metaphorically creeping up those parts of the owner's anatomy more usually reserved for other biological functions.

James Lomas was ambitious. He would stop at nothing to impress the owner and came to believe that one day Mason's Carpet Mill would be his.

Marion, his first wife, aided and abetted. She had been his secretary and had been surprised at his proposal of marriage.

Many were even more surprised at her acceptance. Temporary insanity her own mother had called it. Then, some five years into the marriage, James had arrived home from his morning jog expecting his breakfast to be on the table. When it was not, he was anything but pleased. When Marion failed to respond to his bawling and shouting up the stairs, he galloped up them two at a time. She lay there, quite dead, with a fixed smile on her face.

James was nonplussed. He shook the lifeless body. It was some minutes before he accepted that she had expired. When? He didn't know. Had she already departed this world when he had left the bed half an hour ago? She was cold. And why was she smiling? That he would never know.

"Heart attack," Doctor Mac pronounced on arrival.

James Lomas wore a black tie and cried at the cremation. He was not altogether sure why, unless it was simply because it was the expected form.

After a suitable period of mourning and what seemed a decent passage of time, Bridie O'Mara was installed in the house as house-keeper. She was bending down dusting the skirting boards one day, when James Lomas, unable to control his movements, slipped his hand up her skirt. The girl screamed, reeled round and landed him a blow to the head, and they were married within the month.

It was a mystery to everyone in the village how Bridie O'Mara, a girl with hips as wide as a barrow, was unable to cope with pregnancy. At the third attempt the foetus developed to full term but killed Bridie O'Mara when forcing its way into the world. Because James was unable to fend for himself, let alone a baby, the infant was put up for adoption immediately following the funeral of its mother.

Sarah Ramsbottom was made of sterner stuff. She worked in the weaving shed of Mason's Carpet Mill and though she was chaste and pure, was not afraid to reveal her shapely legs under short skirts. It would be a lucky boy indeed, and on Sarah's part purely an accident, if he caught a glimpse of her cleavage as she bent at the machinery.

James Lomas's ambition was matched only by that of Sarah Ramsbottom. Though he did not know it, she had set her cap at the manager and was not dismayed when she heard he did not like dogs, for wherever Sarah went her dog went too. She played it cool, took her time – just the odd friendly word each morning, the odd smile over the top of the loom, the seemingly innocent condolences whispered over a sandwich at lunchtime. She had a way of making a man think he had done the chasing. It was not long before James Lomas succumbed and they were married before Bridie O'Mara's name had been chiselled into her family headstone.

Meanwhile Mason was not getting any younger. The obsequious James Lomas wheedled his way into the old man's affairs and knew better than the venerable Mason exactly what the firm was worth. It was a surprise to no-one that when old Mason died, having no kith or kin, the Mill was left to James Lomas.

Five weeks of sweeping that yard was enough. As soon as Christmas was over, I bade my farewells to the cobbles and bins in that yard and departed, before the real snows came.

CHAPTER 20

Fear

From my shelter in the hills I could see the fireworks of New Year's Eve sprinkling their myriad stars down from the heavens. The swooshes, and bangs and pops of rockets exploding into the sky carried through the cold, crisp air up into the hills. I stood for a while watching, before I retired into my accommodation which I shared quite willingly with a family of fieldmice.

* * * *

In the usual course of a lifetime most people will experience fear in some form or another. It can be deep and harrowing or brief and shallow, but it will not easily be forgotten.

Myself I have experienced the real thing: it overwhelmed me in waves from my genitals to the top of my head: it devoured my brain and all my senses and I choked on bitter bile that refused to stay down where it should.

Two weeks into the New Year I ventured down into the village. I passed the bakery where the smell of warm bread entertained my nostrils and my stomach began to rumble.

A man the size of a grizzly bear appeared in the doorway of the shop. He had flaming red hair and a full beard to match. In his hand was the remainder of a half loaf which he was devouring hungrily. He wiped his floury hands down the front of his baker's apron and turned to the spade leaning against the wall of the shop. He was shovelling away the snow to make a path on the pavement in front of the shop when he noticed me.

"Want a job?" he asked.

I knew it, I thought. Whenever there's muck to be shovelled people seem to think of me. He held out the spade to me.

"This ain't me usual job – baking and stuff. It's me mate's shop – been tekken bad so I said as I'd help out. Can't let a mate down, can you? But sooner he gets out of his sick-bed the better. Come in when tha's done an' I'll make thee a cuppa."

.... An offer I couldn't refuse.

And true to his word, he had a cuppa waiting for me and warm bread straight from the oven. An old lady was leaving the shop as I entered.

"Thanks, Dennis," she said to him, "and give Cyril my love and say I hope he's soon back."

I sat on a stool at the back of the shop with both hands around the cup to thaw them out.

"How long's tha bin on the road then?" Dennis asked in a broad Yorkshire accent.

In all honesty I could not reply for I kept no account of time.

"Quite a while," I said. "Got made redundant and once the money ran out .."
"Tell me about it," he said sympathetically. "It's not that long ago me and Norma were in dire straits. Every day a struggle for survival – down at the Job Centre where kids were offering me labouring jobs at a pound an hour and telling me I should be glad to take it."

A young, fresh-faced girl came through from the back of the shop.

"I'll be off then, Dennis. Make sure as you lock up."

Dennis nodded. "Sooner Cyril's back the better," he grumbled again. "I'm no good at this lark. Drink up – tha might as well come home wi' me." And before I could ask if his wife might object, he added, "Norma's used to me bringing home lame ducks. Not as you're a lame duck, you understand."

I didn't understand, but he was good company and the prospect of a warm fire out of the snow appealed to me.

"Watch the geese," he warned me as we made our way through dysfunctional tractors in the farm yard that would never function again, "they'll have yer balls as soon as look at thee."

It was obvious that Dennis's fortunes had changed, for the house screamed of *nouveau* wealth. Not for Norma the born-with-a-silver-spoon opulence of Chippendale and Wedgwood; on the mantelpiece were pottery gifts declaring her right to be called "the best grandma in the world" and "a present from Blackpool." Her one concession to good taste was the Bang & Olafsen sound system that took pride of place in the garishly carpeted lounge – the Aga stove in the farmhouse kitchen she had inherited, and although she claimed it was "a bit old fashioned" had kept it because there was still plenty of use left in it.

Dennis knew I must be wondering but would not ask. He sat himself down in a chair covered with plastic sheeting, and said, almost apologetically,

"We won the pools. Me and Norma had allus fancied this here little farm but it was just a dream, you understand – way out of our range even before the mill closed down."

In truth Dennis had once spent a holiday on a farm in Wales where the farmer's wife had let him collect the eggs, but he was soon to learn that there was more to farming than simply collecting eggs. After struggling for a year to raise chickens that refused to lay, he turned the farm into a scrapyard specialising in spares for tractors and other farm machinery, and then he was truly happy.

There was little money about since closure of the mill, but Dennis didn't do it for the money – which was lucky for him because most of his bills were settled in the form of a dozen new-laid eggs, a handful of lavender, a margarine tub of freshly-picked blackberries, and sometimes in promises (that were always kept) to deliver a "nice shoulder of lamb and a few chops when the time comes." His customers were seldom in a hurry. They stayed a while giving and receiving village tittle-tattle, and when they left Dennis would deliver their payments to Norma who would always say, "Good job we don't need the money."

Norma had probably been a beauty in her youth. She still had about her the air and bearing of one who was confident that heads were turning as she passed. Her body was pleasantly rounded, as is often the case just before varicose veins and middle-age spread set in. Standing now on the quarry tiled floor of her kitchen, mistress of her own Aga, in clogs and apron, she flashed a disarming smile at me.

Dennis got up from his plastic-sheet-covered chair.

"He's staying for tea," he told Norma.

I looked at her sheepishly.

"That's if it's okay with you?" I asked.
"What's okay with the boss is okay with me. And I suppose you'll be staying the night in the caravan?"
"Course he will," Dennis confirmed on my behalf. "It's warm lad. I've relayed power to it from the back of the house and there's an electric heater in there."
"I don't know what to say," I said. Norma smiled that disarming smile again.

"I'll get fresh sheets for the bed in there," she said.

Tea, or dinner as they call it south of the Irwell, was delicious – steak and kidney pie with boiled potatoes and carrots. I devoured every morsel without so much as a thought of BSE.

"I'll be off to the pub then, me love," Dennis announced suddenly. I was a little surprised that he didn't invite me, but imagined perhaps my attire would not be appropriate.

"It's his darts night," Norma explained as he left. "I'll show you to the van then."

We crossed the yard, stepping carefully over the innards of various vehicles and avoiding engaging the gaze of any geese that were still about.

"Aren't you bothered about foxes?" I asked Norma as she opened the van door and put on the light.

"It'd be a brave fox that decided to tackle any of them," she replied.

The van was warm. Obviously either she or Dennis had switched on the heater earlier.

"There's a shower here," she said, pointing to a door at the back of the caravan – with clean towels and soap."

I couldn't wait to burrow beneath the clean sheets of that inviting bed. I showered quickly, but thoroughly for it could be the last chance for a while. I shaved with the razor obviously put there for my use. I unwrapped the new toothbrush and cleaned my teeth with minty-fresh Colgate. I sank down under the covers of the deliciously warm bed. I drifted off to the distant strains of Joe Loss emanating from the Bang & Olafsen in the lounge of the farmhouse.

And then I was awake – wide awake. For beside me I felt the smooth silk of bare flesh.

"Did I wake you?" Norma asked mischievously. There was no doubting her intentions, and they were anything but honourable. "Dennis won't be back for ages. Trust me."

Trust didn't come into it. It had been months since I had been this close to a woman. How we came to be on the floor I do not recall, but there I was, pinned down by a naked woman and loving every minute of it.

I had no idea of the time and didn't give Dennis or his kind hospitality a thought. I was betraying his trust with my every move. I eventually collapsed, exhausted. Norma led me back to the bed. She was kneeling on the floor still starkers with her head on my naked chest when the door of the caravan opened, and there stood Dennis.

The word 'fear' took on a whole new meaning. I froze. Then my whole body began to shake. The lights of the caravan were out and his huge figure was silhouetted in the doorway by the lights from the yard.

"Having fun?" he asked.

Norma seemed strangely calm.

"Did you win?" she asked, picking up her knickers from the floor.

"No," he said miserably. This did not bode well for me I feared. Norma pushed past him, knickers in hand.
"Well?" he turned on me. There was no escape: he was in the doorway and I was naked on the bed. I wanted to scream, "I'm sorry, please don't kill me, but I actually said meekly,
"Well, what can I say?"

"You could say whether you enjoyed my Norma or not," he prompted.

Norma called from the kitchen of the house.

"Kettle's on, Dennis, me love. Don't be long."

He was still standing in the doorway, looking at me.

"I think it's time you were on your way," he said.
"I'll get my things," I said, grateful that I was still able to speak and breathe.
"Not tonight, you silly sod," Dennis said. "First light tomorrow. Here's twenty quid to tide you over."

It was obvious to Dennis that the light still hadn't dawned on me, so he felt obliged to explain.

"I love Norma, you understand. But I love Cyril Trumpet more. Norma knows. She understands. But there's many in the village wouldn't." He turned to leave the caravan.
"First light, tha knows," he said, and departed.

The fear leaking out through every pore in my body began to evaporate. But what a fear that had been.

On the steps up to the caravan, I found as I departed at dawn, a neatly parcelled pack of sandwiches. At the end of the lane I turned in time to see the lights coming on in the kitchen of the farmhouse, and pictured Norma there in clogs and apron looking as if butter wouldn't melt in her mouth.

I didn't stop till mid-afternoon. I had walked around ten miles and decided before I looked for shelter for the night to unpack the sandwiches Norma had made me. Tucked between the layers of fresh oven-bottom muffins was a note.

"Thanks," it said.

CHAPTER 21

Full Circle

It was still snowing heavily when I woke up in the barn on High Moor. That night in the cosy little caravan in Dennis's yard seemed a long time ago, though in reality it had been less than a week. The wind was howling through the gaps in the timbers and I decided not to venture out. I pulled my woolly hat down over my ears and lay on my back in my sleeping bag staring up at the joist timbers that supported the roof. At least they were solid. It would take more than a Pennine gale to bring them down on me as I slept.

I lay there a while before I came to my senses ... a tramp might be one thing, but a recluse is another. I was in danger of becoming a recluse. The last time I'd eaten was the last of Norma's sandwiches two days ago. Like it or not, I must venture into the next village, if only to get warm in a public library if there were one there and if I could sneak in without being noticed.

* * * *

There was not a soul in the reading room at the small village library. I had sidled in furtively behind a group of women discussing Joanna Trollope and Catherine Cookson and soon found the quiet place through a door opening with no door. I took a book from a shelf so that if the librarian came upon me I could give the impression I was reading. I had carefully parked my rucksack under the table out of view. Within minutes I was asleep, soothed by the warmth and lulled by the peace.

Unluckily for me it was the library's early closing day and I was aroused by an angry young woman telling me in no uncertain terms that this was not a doss-house. I didn't grace her remark with a reply but gathered up my rucksack and made for the door.

Her colleague at the "Books Out" desk was a bespectacled, elderly lady in twin set and pearls. I imagined, when she made her way round the desk, that she was following me to make sure I left, but as I reached the door to the snow outside, she pressed a couple of coins into my hand.

"Get yourself something to eat," she said. "Tom at The Bull across the road'll see you right." The young girl librarian was approaching, keys in hand.
"She's only young," the elderly lady said apologetically, "she doesn't understand. Think on now – tell Tom that Alice has sent you."

The girl was shouting impatiently.

"Hurry up, Alice. It's time to lock up."

I smiled my thanks to the elderly lady as she shooed me out of the library door.

Across the road at The Bull everyone was shouting, no-one was listening. There was some sort of argument going on in the corner and Tom, the landlord, didn't seem much interested. I put my two coins on the bar top.

"Alice at the Library says you'll find me something," I said. He slid the coins off the counter and put them in the till. Then all hell broke loose in the corner and two ruffians seemed to be getting the better of an elderly man. I am not usually one to interfere, but two against one, and two strong youths at that – well, it's not on.

"He's broken my bloody nose!" one of the youths shouted, wiping blood on his sleeve following my sharp left jab.

"And I'll break more than your bloody nose, if you don't clear off!" I told him and his companion.

"It's not your argument," the youth without bloodied nose protested.

"No matter what the chap's done at you, two of you against him is just not fair. All I'm doing is evening up the odds a bit."

They scarpered. I turned to help the old chap to his feet from the floor where he had dropped, winded from a blow.. The swelling under his eye was already glowing red and would be a real shiner by morning.

"Fred Powers," he said, holding out his hand to me but struggling to stay on his feet. "And I'm grateful to you lad whoever you are."

"They're nowt but thugs," the landlord was saying, giving me a hand steadying old Fred Powers. "They think they can punch their way into and out of anything, but I've barred 'em now, Fred, so tha's no need to fear 'em in here again. We'll all see to that."

The landlord seemed to have forgotten about the money I'd given him and which I'd hoped would be providing at least a pickled egg.

"Hang on," he said though. "You were wanting something to eat, lad, weren't you? I'll get Becky in the back to sort out a sandwich."

"A sandwich!" Fred Powers said, indignantly. "Not on your life – this 'ere lad's coming home with me for a slap-up feed."

"There's really no need ..." I started, hoping he wouldn't believe me.

"That's as maybe, but you're coming all the same. It's nobbut a cockstride away."

Home to Fred was a small farm only half a mile out of the village. The yard, unlike Dennis's which was strewn with broken vehicles, was tidy and well organised.

"We used to be dairy," Fred pointed out on his way past the disused milking parlours, "but we turned to beef now we're older. No to-ing and fro-ing every day with beef – just let 'em eat in a field and keep bugs at bay and they're happy – just sit back and wait for 'em to get fat!"

I knew nothing about farming was as simple as that. He was simply making small talk to make me feel comfortable.

His wife displayed no sign of surprise when the two of us arrived, Fred leaning heavily on me and me trying to keep balance for the two of us on the icy ground. Then she saw the shiner.

"Oh my God!" she said, "what have you done?"
"It's what them two Robinson lads have done, me owd flower. I gave 'em what for, but they were getting the better of me when this 'ere chap turned up and gave 'em what for." He chuckled. He went over to his wife and kissed her, "So I think he deserves a bed for the night, don't you?"

In the morning I rose early, rolled up the clean clothes that Fred's wife had washed and left airing on an overhead rack, thanked her for her hospitality and set off through the yard. At the end of the yard, Fred was puffing and panting, swinging a heavy axe, chopping logs. I put the rucksack down on the snow.

"Give us that here, Fred," I said. "I'll get it done for you."

The old man stood up, put his hands on his waist and stretched backwards. "My old bones aren't what they used to be," he said. And then he saw the rucksack on the ground. "You're not for leaving us so soon, are you?" he asked with disappointment in his voice. "Clara and I were both hoping you'd stay a while. We could use some help about the place – but that's not the only reason – we thought you might be glad of warm shelter till the worst of this weather is over."

For one with such an intense dislike of farming, I always seemed to be ending up mucking out some animal or other. But I looked at Fred's face – a flushed, wrinkled, kind face…

To my own surprise, collecting eggs and mending fences and re-building fallen walls, swilling down the yard and taking fodder out to the cattle did not seem unpleasant at all; perhaps it was because the company was so engaging. I became very fond of the old couple and wondered if, when the snows finally melted, I would have the courage to leave them.

They'd met, Fred and Clara, at a Young Farmer's do at the local church hall some forty-two years ago. They had been blessed with twin boys, but neither had taken to farming. One had emigrated to Australia where he worked on computers and the other had married a flamenco dancer while on holiday in Spain and now had five children, none of whom spoke English and none of whom had ever met their grandparents.

They were a kind, hard-working couple and each day I grew closer and closer to them.

The snows began to melt and soon there were only pockets of dirty yellow and grey slush left in the hollows where the winter sun could not penetrate. When new snow did fall, it quickly dissolved into the ground, and I began to think I should move on.

Towards the end of March when the coltsfoot was beginning to push through the earth by the hedgerows, I sat with Fred on the wall at the end of the farm yard, eating the sandwiches Clara had made for our lunch and drinking hot tea from a Thermos.

"Do you ever miss home?" Fred asked quite suddenly.
"I don't have a home," I replied simply.

"Then this is your home, lad," he said quietly, "for as long as you want."

He was silent, waiting for some sort of response from me.

"We used to have a beach house in Cornwall," I told him. "Years ago. Seems a lifetime ago. I wonder sometimes if it's still there. That's all."

"Then why don't you take a break and go and find out?" he said. "We'll find the fare if that's all that's stopping you. But mind," and he looked me straight in the eyes, "the ticket would be a two-way ticket and we'd expect you back, you understand?"

I had the money for the fare. My "wages" were small for they were not wealthy people, but I had no need of money for they provided my food and shelter and clothing.

Spring in Cornwall, as I've said before, is like mid-summer in the Pennines. There was blossom on the trees and flowers in the grass and a scent of pure air teased my nostrils. I sat outside a cafe writing a postcard to Fred and Clara... *Weather glorious, digs good but food not in the same class as yours Clara. Old beach house is still there, just about! See you soon.*

I was actually missing them – me, independent, free-as-a-bird, self-contained me – I was missing Fred's old jokes and Clara's apple pie.

As I stood up to leave, I crashed my seat into a wheelchair parked by a table behind me.
"I'm so sorry," I said.
"My fault," she said, "for being so close to your chair."

I knew the voice, the gentle Cornish lilt. I saw the hands smoothing down her skirt, and I knew the hands. If there were wrinkles on the face I did not see them. If there was sadness in the voice I did not hear it. I saw only a beautiful woman I had once loved and whose memory had warmed me on many chilly nights in draughty barns.

I sat back down on the chair so that my eyes would be at her level, and I took her hands.

"Jean," I said, "it's…"
"I know," she said, her hand going to her hair and twirling it nervously as she had done in that yesterday of my memory.

The years rolled away. It was as if the intervening years had melted into oblivion and we were sitting on the cliff top bench again, looking out to sea and eating lunch. My mind swam in the luxury of her presence and my heart thumped against my chest. When I could eventually find words, it was to ask if she'd stay and have another coffee with me ... of all the things I wanted to say, why had it come out so mundane?

"I have all the time in the world," she said. "All the time in the world to listen to what's been happening to you."
"No," I said emphatically on returning from the cafe counter where I had ordered coffees, "there is little to tell of me, but there is so much I want to know about you."

Her marriage had not lasted long. Some months after losing a child she had become ill. At her mother's insistence she went to see her doctor who referred her to a consultant. She knew it would be but a matter of time before she would be confined to a wheelchair, but she delayed telling her husband, for she knew he would never cope. He could not deal with illness of any kind – he believed it was a weakness to be ill. She learned three years after their divorce that he had suffered a stroke and she had wondered how on earth he would cope with that.

Neither of us touched the fresh coffee that was delivered to our table. We sat holding hands and such was the intensity of our feelings that we neither of us wanted to let the other go.

A car drew up at the pavement near to where we were sitting.

"Dad – come to collect me," Jean said.

I'd never met her parents and for a grown man I was strangely nervous. I needn't have been. I asked him to allow me to lift Jean into the car. He smiled.

"There's plenty of room in the back," he offered. "Get in. I feel as if I know you."

I checked out of my digs the next morning and took up Jean's invitation to spend the rest of the week with her at her parents' house. They were kindly people who did not regard Jean as a burden, but believed caring for loved ones to be a privilege.

"I want to help," I insisted. "Please show me how to care for her."

They could tell, as anyone could, by simply seeing us together how close our bond was: after such a long time and so short a relationship, it amazed even me that our bond had not only survived but had strengthened.

The night before I was due to return to Yorkshire, I sat down with Jean's father.
"What would you say, if I asked if I could take Jean home with me – to Yorkshire? There is no-one in the world I would rather spend the rest of my life with. I've travelled about, almost lost – some would say I've been a tramp, a vagrant, a down-and-out. But I am honest and I am settled now with kind, caring folk who would welcome us into their home."

He puffed on his pipe and rocked back in the chair.

"Can I think on it?" he asked.

I nodded.

That night I walked along the cliff top to where the wooden bench had been where Jean and I had first met. There was *graffiti* scribbled on the broken and splintered planks that formed the seat. I sat there and looked out to sea, where lights from fishing boats sparkled in the distance, flickering in and out as the boats bobbed on the tide.

When I thought I had given Jean's parents time to talk, I made my way back, calling at the telephone box on the corner of the street.

"Fred," I said, "I've met an old friend down here ..."
"The answer's yes, of course," he said.

"You don't know what I'm going to say," I said. But he did. Up in Yorkshire he was smiling a knowing smile.

"Remember I confided in you once about a girl I'd met in Cornwall?"

There were tears the day after of course, when Jean and I made ready for our journey north. Jean had been the biggest part of their lives and life was going to be different for them now.

"You must follow your heart," they had always told her, and now they did not resent her doing just that.

"We'll visit often," I promised them, "and of course you will visit us."

Her mother hugged me.

"Take care of my child," she begged rather than instructed.

"She is as precious to me," I assured her, "as she is to you. Nothing in the world can come between us ever again. I promise you both I shall make her happy."

My homecoming to Yorkshire was eagerly awaited by Fred and Clara. They had made ready for us the big double bed that I had slept in since my arrival there. The smell of hot bread reached us across the yard, and Clara came out running, arms outstretched, to engulf me in a warm embrace.

"Let's get you inside, me love," she said to Jean, taking charge of the wheelchair. As we unpeeled clothing that we had not needed at the start of our journey in Cornwall but certainly needed against the Pennine spring, Clara prepared one of her delicious dinners.

Fred came in from the fields and greeted us both warmly.

They were both enchanted by Jean, as I had been when first we met. From the very moment of her arrival, there had been no doubt in their minds that she would be staying.

I did not close the curtains of the bedroom to. I deliberately left them open so that I could see Jean by the light of the moon that filtered into the room, to assure myself throughout the night that I was not dreaming. I lifted Jean onto the bed and gently slid in beside her. The yesterdays on the cliff top came flooding back into my mind and I sank into a warm and happy sleep.

For one who had once hated farming, it is remarkable that I settled into this life with consummate ease. I sang in the fields, in the bath, in the bed.

Sometimes Jean and I would lie in the big double bed in silence, words being unnecessary. And sometimes we would talk throughout the night. And always we were happy in each other's arms.

So happy were we in fact that I sometimes feared it could not last and something terrible would happen. But it seems that Jean and I had paid in advance, for one day when I returned from the fields with Fred and a wayward bull in tow and Clara singing in the kitchen, I came upon my beloved Jean standing between the timbers of the doorway. Standing. Unaided, and glowing as only she ever glowed in my eyes.

I guess somewhere along the way I must have done something right, but exactly how I had earned such happiness will always be a mystery to me. On Sundays now I attend the chapel that I had scorned in my early days with Edna. On my knees I give thanks – for the Robinson boys who were duffing up Fred when I came to his aid and without which incident I would never have finished up here – and for the love of my life who kneels there beside me – and whom I will strive for the rest of my days to deserve.

THE END